Tarzan &

Janine

Published by Story Ink LLC
ISBN-13: 9781626950016
ISBN-10: 1626950016

Tarzan & Janine

~ Texas Billionaires Club ~

Delilah Devlin
&
Elle James

Story Ink LLC

To our mom, who never stopped nagging
us to finish this story!

Chapter One

"Holy Hell." Tanner Peschke groaned.

"My friend, you worry far too much." Rip O'Rourke grinned from across the table but stared through the barroom door.

Tanner rolled his eyes. Rip didn't look as though he had a care in the world—the eye-straining Hawaiian shirt paired with his beat-up cowboy hat pretty much reflected his whole outlook on life.

"Wow, T-man. You couldn't have picked a better place for us to meet."

"I should have known this was a set up." Tanner ran a hand through his hair and stared out into the Austin, Texas hotel lobby hosting the National Beauty Products Convention. "My old man is testing me."

Rip sighed. "This place is heaven."

"It's hell for me." Tanner waved a hand at the plethora of women—slim, curvy, tall, petite, fresh-faced, mature—and in every mouth-watering color scheme available on the planet. "Look at them. All of them. I'll never make the deal he expects."

"Tanner, why don't you just tell your father you quit?" Jesse Jordan sipped his steaming coffee.

The twinkle in his eye said he understood

Tanner's predicament all too well. Although women fawned over the young Robert Redford lookalike, he didn't melt like hot wax.

"You don't need Peschke Motors," Jesse said. "You make more on your investments in a month than that place sees in a year."

"I made a promise to my mother—"

"On her deathbed ten years ago." Gage Jenkins, a no-nonsense man with a military haircut and direct stare, leaned over the table. "Dude, a lot has changed since then."

"You could buy ten Peschke Motors with your pocket change." Rip shook his head. "Hell, you could probably buy your own new car manufacturing company with the money you're making in day trading."

"That's not the point." Tanner leaned back in his seat. "Why do you work at the radio station, Rip?" Irritation tightened his throat. He turned to Jesse and waved a hand. "Why do you run a ranch supply store, Jess? And why are you still a member of the Army National Guard, Gage?" Tanner glanced around at the group. "None of us do what we do because we *need* the money."

"That's right." Rip let out a belch, followed by a grin. "Sorry."

Tanner shook his head. "We started the Texas Billionaires Club so we would all succeed."

Rip nodded. "And once we made our

collective billion, we are supposed to remind each other what's important."

"Family, friends and, most important, not getting a big head." Jesse counted off, one finger at a time.

"Back to the point." Gage set his coffee mug on the table with a thump. "Tanner made a promise...to his dying mother, who is family, to stand by his father...who is family."

"That's why I called this meeting, my friends." Tanner straightened his collar. "I needed moral support and a reminder of what's important. My dad's counting on me to do this right."

"Well, soldier." Gage threw back his broad shoulders and gave Tanner his best military glare. "Get out there and make that deal."

"I don't get it." Rip's brows furrowed. "What's so hard about buying a load of used cars from an old lady?"

"He's a sucker for a sob story." Jesse shook his head, a grin spreading across his mouth. "This place is filled with women, a veritable field of land mines for our man Tanner."

"You got that right." Tanner stood, staring out at the lobby, dread filling him with each passing second.

Jesse, Gage and Rip stood, Rip leaning in like a quarterback in a huddle. "Keep your eye on the ball. Ignore the other team, and the fact you'll be surrounded and outnumbered by the fairer sex."

"Thanks," Tanner snorted. "I'm ignoring them already." His tone dripped sarcasm.

"You can do it, buddy." Rip pounded him on his back. "Just pretend they're all men in drag and breeze right through."

"We've got your back." Jesse took his turn pounding Tanner's back. "Call us when you're done. We'll give you a cyber high-five."

"I'm on it." Tanner strode out of the bar and entered the lobby. Knowing the TBC had his back gave him fuel to get going.

On his way to the reception desk, several lovelies nodded, smiling as they passed. Others fluttered their fingers in little feminine waves—the kind that made a man's insides curl. All the while, the combined scents of their perfumes increased the dread in his sensory-overloaded brain.

Tanner cleared his throat and straightened his red tie. Time to get serious. This meeting was important to his father's business and crucial to Tanner's future at Peschke Motors. The appointment could be the beginning of bigger and better things...or the beginning of the end.

Passing a large gilt-framed mirror, he checked his appearance. He'd been shooting for honest and down-to-earth to appeal to the matriarch and CEO of Barbara Stockton's Beauty Secrets. Thus the blue chambray shirt, crisply ironed blue jeans, and highly polished cowboy boots. Next to all the beautifully groomed and fashionably dressed women in attendance at the conference, he probably looked like a hick. He got great pleasure in knowing he wasn't just a hick. He had money. Lots of money, but he chose not to advertise that fact. No one in Texas but his banker knew exactly how much money he had. And he liked the situation that way.

Tanner usually didn't give much thought to what he wore or how others viewed him, but his normally take-me-as-I-am attitude had gone for a hike after his father's latest challenge, which he'd delivered just that morning...

"Son, if you're gonna run this company when I retire, you've gotta show me you want it."

That was the hard part. Tanner really didn't want the business. He didn't have Jesse's steadiness, Gage's laser-focus, or even Rip's laissez-faire attitude. He was a man approaching thirty and feeling strangled in place because he hadn't found his life's calling.

Sitting across the desk from his father, Tanner silently groaned and tipped his cowboy hat forward so his dad couldn't detect his impatience. He knew he was in for his father's latest lecture on "Used Car Sales Business: Lecture Number 4123."

Try as he might, he couldn't force the passion his father had for the sales game. But Tanner promised his mother on her deathbed that he'd help his father with the family business. He wished he'd inherited his father's natural used-car-salesman gene. The fact was, he hadn't.

Just once, he'd like hearing his father's praise and admiration of his business prowess. But his father wouldn't sugarcoat what wasn't there for him to see at Peschke Motors.

Too often, Tanner bit hard on his tongue to keep from telling his father he didn't need him or the job or anything to do with Peschke Motors. But his sweet mother's last words always came back. "Take care of your father. Help him. He needs you."

"Tanner!" Joe Peschke's booming voice pricked the bubble of Tanner's memory. "Son, are you payin' attention to anything I'm sayin'?"

"Yes, sir," Tanner lied and decided he'd better give the man his undivided attention, or this could turn into an even longer ordeal than usual. By the look of his father's ruddy cheeks and bristling black moustache, Tanner guessed he'd missed a cue.

His dad rose to his feet, his bulky frame towering over Tanner. "I plan on buyin' a fishin' boat and a house on the beach. In exactly three months, I'm movin' there. Do you understand what I'm sayin'?"

Tanner must have drifted *way* off. This was the first he'd heard about his father moving. "You're moving?"

"Yes, I'm moving."

"But how will you run the business from the coast?"

"I'm won't. I'm retirin'."

"Retiring?" This was new, too.

"Yes, and I wanted to leave the family business in the hands of family. I had high hopes that family would be you, seein' as you're the only family I have left."

Tanner pushed his hat back on his head, every fiber of his being tuned in to his dad's words. He could feel a "but" coming...

"But, I need a quarterback who can lead the team to victory. Problem is, son, I'm just not seein' you as that quarterback."

Wait a minute. Tanner couldn't have heard that right. "You mean, you'd fire me?" he asked disbelieving. A little devil in his conscience leapt for joy, while an angel with a face like his mother's shook her head sadly.

"Not necessarily fire you, but I need to select a general manager. If you're not the man for the job, I can't put you in it."

7

A cold, hard lump lodged in Tanner's throat. Perhaps now was the time to break it to his father that he was a multi-millionaire and didn't need the job of general manager. But that time had come and gone. Telling his father he didn't need him might break the old man's heart and would definitely go against what Tanner had promised his mother. Caught between a rock and a soft spot, Tanner argued, "I've sold fifteen cars in the last month, Dad. How many other salesmen have sold as many?"

Joe Peschke shook his head, his mouth turned down in a sad frown. "Not a one. Volume's not your problem, son."

"Then what is?"

His father lifted a piece of paper from the stack on his desk and shook it. "Statistics show every car you sold to a woman, you sold *at*, or a fraction above, cost. Which barely pays the bills around here, much less your commission."

Tanner knew he couldn't refute his father's words. "But Dad, you don't understand."

His father shook the paper. "Then help me understand, son." Scanning down the list, he poked a finger at a line. "The green conversion van."

"That would be Mrs. Jenkins." Tanner straightened his shoulders. "Her husband's disabled and they live on a fixed income."

His father frowned and looked farther down the list. "How about that blue, four-door Saturn?"

"Rebecca Pitkin." Tanner remembered the frazzled redhead with the toddler. "Student. Single mom. Needed reliable transportation to get her daughter to daycare. She's trying to make a better life for herself and her child."

With a roll of his eyes, the older Peschke went to the next line. Crossing his arms over his chest, his father slowly shook his head. "Tell me about the F-150 Pickup."

Tanner groaned inwardly. Was this how a frog pinned to a dissecting board felt? "F-150 pickup?" Damned if he could remember the face that went with that vehicle. "Refresh my memory, Dad."

"Micky Freeland ring a bell?"

"Micky... wasn't that a man?"

"I don't know too many men who dot their 'i's with hearts."

"I could have sworn she was a man," Tanner muttered. A sick feeling filled his stomach. His father was right.

Tossing the paper back in the pile on his desk, his father leaned forward. "Truth is, son, you're a marshmallow with the women."

"And that's a crime?" Tanner knew the answer before the words left his lips.

"In the used car business, it is. We're not a charity organization." His father leaned back in his chair, pinching the bridge of his nose. "The word is out. You sold three cars to three generations of Smithson women. And they'll all be tellin' their friends."

"That could be a good thing." *C'mon, Tanner, spin this in your favor.* "Return customers and word-of-mouth advertising is bound to be good for business."

"Won't do the dealership a darn bit of good, if they're all comin' to you, son." His father shook his head, his lips tightening. "Face facts—as soon as a female feeds you a sob story, you're silly putty in her hands."

Tanner hung his head, knowing every word his father spoke was true. He was a soft touch where women were concerned. That wily Smithson grandmother had him pegged the moment they'd met.

For just a moment, he'd held her hand, feeling the parchment-thin skin and smelling the lilac fragrance she'd doused herself in. He hadn't been able to bear the thought of the elderly pensioner making high payments for the vehicle she had her heart set on. Hell, Tanner didn't need the commission. He could subsidize every one of their customers if the action didn't leave a paper trail back to his investment portfolio.

"I have no complaints about your sales

volume. You need to work on your profit margin if you want to prove you have the fire in your belly for this business."

Right now, the only fire Tanner felt in his belly was the ulcer he'd earned. Despite the promise he'd made to his mother, he still resisted committing the rest of his life to Peschke Motors.

"You've got three months. Make those months count. And, son, decide what you're gonna do with your life." His father had leaned his forearms on the desk to deliver the final warning. "Don't straddle that fence—all you'll get is bruised balls."

At two o'clock that same afternoon, Tanner was feeling pretty bruised all right. Standing in line at the concierge's desk in the hotel lobby, his stomach still roiled at his father's words. Even knowing he had the support of his best buddies wasn't helping.

Barbara Stockton of Barbara Stockton's Beauty Secrets, or BS-Squared as he thought of her, had requested him specifically for this deal, and that he come to her. Tanner hoped like hell she wasn't Aggie Smithson's friend. This was his chance to make the deal of a lifetime. A chance to redeem himself for all the missed opportunities—if he could keep a hard-core business mind and not be swayed by a woman's woes.

"I'm here to meet with Barbara Stockton. Could you tell me what room she's in?" he asked the busy concierge.

"I'll have to call her room first to verify the appointment. Could you wait just a moment, sir?"

"Sure, I'll wait over there." Tanner pointed toward a potted plant set next to an entryway.

Women moved in surges, ebbing and flowing from the ballroom. Feeling out of place and outnumbered, he swam with the current until he reached the plant. He almost grabbed hold to keep from being swept into the sea of estrogen. More than once, he could swear he felt the soft pat of a hand on his ass.

Tanner stared into the ballroom from his anchoring tree, feeling incongruous as the only male for as far as his eyes could see. The large expanse was partitioned into dozens of booths where women demonstrated various beauty products. Hands in his pockets, Tanner forced himself to relax. He leaned against the doorframe and heaved a sigh.

Why were women his greatest weakness? What about them made him such a pushover? Every last one of them—be they homely or gorgeous, elderly or eligible—left him feeling like he had to protect them, take care of them, and ease their worries. Why did they have that affect on him, and how could he armor himself against it to pull off this deal?

He had a knack for bringing in the customers. Perhaps he should stick to publicity and marketing and let someone else handle the sales. He certainly wasn't helping the dealership if he gave away cars. And Peschke Motors had been a part of the Peschke family for three generations. The place meant a lot to his father, therefore, the business meant a lot to Tanner.

How could he make his father proud and keep the business going? Ideas raced through his head, none seemed substantial enough to impress his father.

"Please notice when Rafael applies the Miracle Hairspray, it goes on evenly, without spitting or clogging."

Tanner heard her before he saw her. Though soft and breathy, the voice carried over the steady hum of hundreds of feminine conversations. And that voice made every hair on his body stand up and cry *halleluiah*.

Because he stood a good foot above the tallest, he didn't have to crane his neck to see over the heads of the women gathered.

A beauty perched on a stool with a mini-microphone attached to the low-cut lapel of her suit jacket.

"Holy hell," Tanner breathed.

When the spraying stopped, the woman climbed gracefully from the high stool and shook her hair back from her shoulders. "See? Every hair remains in place with a springy, natural hold."

Tanner's gaze remained riveted—but not only to her hair. Her entire package captivated him from the top of her golden blonde coif to the tips of her bright pink, Barbie-style stilettos. Every curve and feature in perfect proportion, her beauty was reminiscent of Marilyn Monroe. And that musical, breathy voice made his pulse flutter and his mouth dry. Tanner's blood raced from his heart to his extremities—one in particular.

The cotton-candy pink suit that would have looked feminine but professional on any other woman, clung lovingly to her generous curves. The skirt ended just above her knees—round, pink kissable knees. The three-inch stilettos emphasized delicate ankles and well-defined calves. But just her physical perfection wasn't what drew him, she dripped sweetness.

Tanner gulped and forced himself to look beyond the woman to the enraptured crowd gathering around her. With her voice, beauty and natural talent, she could sell beachfront property in Arizona. *Or...*

A Cadillac of an idea slipped into Tanner's mind and gunned all eight cylinders.

This gifted, eloquent and drop-dead-gorgeous woman could be the answer to all his prayers. But who was she?

Tanner stepped forward, but pressure on his arm stopped him, and he looked to the source.

"Excuse me, sir." The concierge stood at his elbow, drawing his attention from his salvation. "Ms. Stockton will see you now in the Double Diamond suite. It's on the forty-sixth floor—the first door on your right when you exit the elevator."

"Thank you very much." Tanner turned to treat himself to one last glimpse of the curvaceous blond in the pink suit. "I'll talk with you later," he whispered before heading for the elevator and the dreaded meeting with BS-Squared.

The trip to the forty-sixth floor took only three minutes. Not much time to compose his scattered thoughts. Thankfully, the fifty-something-year-old Ms. Stockton couldn't possibly hold as much appeal as the breathy blonde who waited below. And she wasn't old enough to play to his soft side, like the infamous Aggie Smithson.

Tanner rapped lightly against the door bearing the shiny brass nameplate with "Double Diamond Suite" engraved in bold letters.

When the door opened, he turned up his smile full force. "Hello, I'm Tanner Peschke, you must be..." Tanner's voice faded and his smile slipped.

"Barbara Stockton," she finished for him. "Won't you come in?" Turning, she stepped aside and waved a hand with a flourish, indicating the way.

He gulped, and his heart sank to his knees. "I'm doomed."

"Pardon me, did you say something, Tanner? You don't mind my calling you Tanner, do you?" Barbara Stockton's throaty voice purred. She eyed him with a raised eyebrow and a knowing smile.

"I said, nice room." Edging past her, he entered the lioness's den.

For a woman in her fifties, Barbara Stockton was very well preserved. Her shoulder-length, dark brown hair curled artistically around her face and glinted with beautifully engineered red and gold highlights. She wore a full-length wrap made of a filmy leopard print. Beneath it, she sported a black sports-bra and figure-hugging leopard-print leggings. And if that wasn't enough, the black thong worn over the leggings was the clincher.

Tanner frowned. This was no Aggie Smithson. Barbara Stockton was a very astute businesswoman, a lion in the jungle of gone-by-the-wayside beauty products distributors. What did he have to fear? She didn't inspire him to one iota of protectiveness. If anything, he felt like raw meat being dangled to entice her ravenous appetite.

Pushing back his shoulders, he stood tall, schooling his face into that of a professional businessman. Tanner was sure even a seasoned negotiator like his dad would have difficulty with this feline. With a raised eyebrow, he said in his smoothest voice, "I'll wait by the window while you get dressed."

He could handle this. Barbara's beauty didn't appeal to him. But the blonde downstairs did, and he couldn't wait to return to the ballroom to propose his idea for the dealership.

"Daahhling, you seem awfully tense." Barbara's voice tickled the back of Tanner's ear as her fingers dug into the taut muscles at the base of his neck. "*Relaaaxxxx.*"

Tanner inhaled deeply, but it didn't work. How could a man relax when a cat had her claws in him?

"It's awfully warm in here, don't you think? I just finished working out." She slipped the filmy wrap from her sleek, well-toned shoulders and the garment cascaded to the floor in a careless heap. With a practiced turn, she walked toward a cabinet on the far wall. "Can I pour you a drink?"

Think blonde, think blonde. His new mantra had the immediate effect of bringing to mind the pretty spokeswoman in the ballroom downstairs. Thinking of the two women, Tanner realized no comparison existed.

Granted, Barbara Stockton was incredibly hot, but she didn't have the same impact. Her moves were too predatory, too calculated. A feral cougar, he could resist.

"Yes, I'd like a drink." Tanner eased his mouth into a genuine smile, feeling more confident by the moment.

"What's your poison?" she asked with a little flirty glance from beneath her brown eyelashes.

"Whiskey." He smiled wider, confidence restored, a feeling of invulnerability spiking his blood.

With his 'Marilyn' firmly fixed in his mind, he spent the next two hours playing musical chairs among the sofas and loveseats in the suite, while negotiating the purchase of a fleet of cotton-candy pink company cars from the equally determined CEO.

By the end of the meeting, Tanner had won. He'd gotten BS-Squared's handshake—and unsolicited kiss—on a contract that promised the dealership a tidy return once they'd repainted and sold the vehicles. The contract was a coup de grace, and he hadn't had to compromise the company, or himself, to get it.

Exiting BS-Squared's suite with a

promise from her to visit the lot, Tanner allowed a little strut in his stride as he returned to the ballroom. He was determined to find "Marilyn". During his time with BS-Squared, he'd begun to think of the blonde as his good luck charm. Somehow, he had to convince her to come to work for Peschke Motors.

Once inside the ballroom, he was disappointed when he didn't see her at the Miracle Spray booth. After five minutes of scanning the multitude in the area, he finally spotted her on a raised dais, astride a mechanical bull.

She'd changed her clothing. Body-hugging denim and gray snakeskin boots were topped with a scoop-necked pale pink T-shirt that ended just above her silver belt buckle.

"As you can see, even a full two hours after applying Miracle Hairspray, my hairstyle is still in place."

Tanner was fascinated. He hadn't imagined the sexy, breathy voice. Nor had he exaggerated the impact of her voluptuous figure. She spoke with the confidence of an experienced actress and, even more intriguing and definitely arousing, she rode the mechanical bull like a pro.

With a hand gripping the rope tied around the torso of the beast, she held her other arm high in the air in true rodeo-rider fashion. Each rise and fall caused the woman's breasts to lift and dip. That little space of skin between her tiny T-shirt and her belt played peek-a-boo with her audience.

God Bless America—and the inventor of the mechanical bull. Every red-white-and-blue blood cell in Tanner's body rode south. Without thinking, he crossed the ballroom floor and climbed onto the dais. He had to talk to her now.

"Even a bucking bull can't destroy the beauty and natural spring." Janine Davis recited her scripted lines without fail. Maybe this wasn't an Academy Award-winning performance, but she gave it her all anyway. Every acting job added a credit to her resume, putting her one step closer to realizing her dream.

"Ma'am, I don't think the hairspray has anything to do with your beauty."

The voice from behind startled her into forgetting her lines and temporarily losing her balance. The bull dipped, and she started to slip. She dropped her arm and grabbed the rough hemp rope encircling the bucking bull.

When she'd righted herself, she glared at the tall man at her side. "Please don't talk to me, sir."

"What if I have a question about the product?" he countered, a smile curving his mouth.

Taking another dip, she loosened her grip and pressed her free hand to the microphone on her lapel. "I have a script to follow, and you're not in it. Please don't distract me," she whispered fiercely, loud enough for him to hear, but not for other conventioneers passing by. She forced a bright smile, directing it toward the audience.

"Pardon me, ma'am. I wouldn't dream of keeping you from your job."

Her gaze narrowed, but he didn't appear to be mocking her. "Good. Now please move along before you get me fired." Janine scanned the room full of people, looking for her boss, before returning her gaze to the man beside her.

He was kind of cute. Tall and dark with a grin that could melt a girl's bones into a gooey puddle. He spread his large hands wide, an innocent look on his smiling face. "Now, how could I get you fired? You're positively brilliant."

Exasperated by his persistence, and at herself for getting all tingly when he was near, she replied, "All I know is I need this job to make my rent money, so don't blow it for me."

"All right, but first tell me your name." He leaned back against the bull's control panel and crossed one ankle over the other.

The man's brown-black eyes held a wicked gleam she found hard to resist. "Janine Davis. Why do you ask?" she said, fighting hard not to notice how sexy he was because the bull's rhythmic motions jounced her breasts and drove her lower parts hard against the saddle. Sensations she had no business noticing began to build along with the thrumming heat flooding her veins.

"I wanted to know the name of the woman I need to thank."

Curiosity won out. Her annoyance at his interruption forgotten for the moment, her head tilted to the side as she continued rocking back and forth on the bull. "Thank me? Why?"

"Because of you, I made the best deal imaginable with old BS-Squared herself."

"Who's BS-Squared?" she asked.

"Barbara Stockton of Barbara Stockton's Beauty Secrets. You know—B. S. B. S..."

Janine frowned.

"Two BS's is BS-Squared." He shook his head. "Never mind. You're my new good luck charm. I just made the best deal of my career."

A movement behind the gorgeous cowboy caught Janine's attention, and her heart nearly stopped. Her boss was headed her way. With her hand squashing the microphone to her breast, Janine whispered,

"Uh, sir, don't look now, but..." She jerked her head in his direction.

He ignored her attempt to interrupt and continued, "So you see, I have you to thank for keeping my mind on business with old BS-Squared."

Janine cringed. Why hadn't he taken her hint and shut the hell up? She let go of the rope around the bull's middle and waved, pasting a smile on her stiff lips. "I wouldn't thank me now," she sang.

"Why?" The tall man's eyes widened and his jaw slackened. His gaze locked with Janine's. "She's right behind me, isn't she?"

"Uh huh." Janine nodded. "Uh...hi there, Ms. Stockton." She bit the corner of her lip and fluttered her fingers in a strained attempt at a light-hearted greeting.

The cowboy swung around, his elbow knocking against a lever on the control panel.

The bull leapt into high speed.

Janine squealed and grasped for the rope—for something to hold on to—but her hands flailed uselessly in the air.

After three raucous bucks, the bull spun, knocking the man from the stage to land flat on his butt on the floor in front of Barbara Stockton. At least he'd earned his just desserts.

Janine smirked and would have clapped her hands if she weren't in trouble herself.

The bull jerked one direction, then lurched and spun another, flinging Janine through the air.

She screamed and twisted, attempting to land on her feet. Instead, she fell face-first on top of the man who'd caused all this.

"Ooomph!" Their chests met with enough force to knock the wind out of them both. Stunned, and fighting for her breath, Janine resisted the urge to hide her face against the cowboy's broad chest. She wished a gigantic black hole would open up and suck in her humiliated self.

Unfortunately, Janine felt the intensity of her boss's glare before she pushed up on her hands and turned to smile sheepishly. "See? The hairspray holds even through the worst of conditions."

Ms. Stockton's expression was not amused. "My, my, isn't this touching. The hired help flirting with the used car salesman."

Janine had a gut feeling the tightness on the older woman's face did not bode well. Turning her anger to the cause of this debacle, she glared down at the man lying beneath her.

When Janine looked down at Tanner, all he could think about was her thighs straddling the only un-stunned part of his body. Her full, rounded breasts pressed intimately against his chest.

Barbara Stockton's outraged expression didn't even faze him when Janine struggled to sit up. He could feel himself harden in response to her denim-covered bottom rubbing against his groin. How much torture could a man take and survive?

A clicking noise next to his ear finally got his attention. The sound was a shoe tapping against the floor—Ms. Stockton's shoe. When his gaze made the trip up the long sleek legs of his client to rest on her angry face, his stomach plunged.

"This whole scene reeks of low class. And I make it a habit to deal only with high-class operations..." BS-Squared's eyebrows rose as she stared pointedly at him, then turned to Janine, "...and individuals. I'm afraid your services are no longer required, Miss Davis. Collect your wages and get out of my sight."

"But Ms. Stockton—" Janine pushed to a sitting position astride Tanner.

A pretty little frown making her even more adorable in Tanner's books.

The CEO held her hand up. "Just leave."

A wad of guilt twisted in Tanner's gut.

"And, Mr. Peschke?" BS-Squared's lips moved with careful, cutting precision. "The deal is off." Executing a perfect about-face, she left the room and the disaster Tanner had created in her wake.

Tanner groaned and let his head flop back against the floor, welcoming the slight pain. His dad was going to kill him.

"Thanks for nothing, mister." Janine finally got her feet beneath her and rose.

Tanner stood and flashed a scowl at the crowd gathered around them, and they quickly dispersed. He turned to Janine. "I'm sorry about that. Hitting that switch was an accident."

"As far as I'm concerned, you're a walking accident looking for a place to happen." Her words were clipped and angry. "Now, what am I going to do? This was the best-paying acting job I've had in a while."

That was his cue. If he wanted to keep his good luck charm, boost profits and do it his way, he had to convince Janine to go along with his plan.

Brushing off his hand against the side of his leg, he held it out. He gave her the smile his grandmother had told him could *tempt the birds from the trees*. "Janine Davis, have I got a deal for you."

Chapter Two

Joe Peschke checked his watch, memorized the placement of the checkers, and rose from the game table. "It's time. I'll put on the television if you'll get the beer."

Bartholomew Biacowski, known to his friends as 'Beans', short for bean pole on account of his tall, slim frame, stood and lazily stretched then scratched his little potbelly.

Joe wasn't fooled. He'd seen Beans glance slyly at the game before heading to the kitchen. Keeping sight of the table from the corner of his eye, Joe flipped through the channels to the local television station where he regularly bought advertising time. Tanner had promised the commercial would run right before the late night newscast. Joe relaxed when Beans returned without finding some excuse to stop by the game table first.

Beans handed a beer to Joe and then settled into one of the matching armchairs in front of the fifty-two-inch television Joe had splurged on prior to the previous year's Super Bowl game. "So, what did Tanner say this ad was gonna be like?"

"He didn't. Said it was a surprise, and that I'd like it." Joe rolled his eyes and shot a doubtful grin in Beans's direction. "Tanner's been doin' live ads for the dealership for the past two years, and I haven't liked a single one."

"Why ya lettin' him do them, then?"

"I don't know. I guess 'cause it gives him somethin' he thinks he's doin' well. It makes him happy."

"How long you gonna mollycoddle that boy, Joe?" Beans took a long pull from his beer.

"I promised Judith on her deathbed, I'd look out for him."

"Yeah, but I'm sure she meant until he was growed. That boy's twenty-eight. By most people's standards—a man. When ya gonna stop wipin' his butt for him and make him stand on his own two feet?"

"Yesterday." Joe smiled. "You'd a been proud of me, Beans. I finally put the screws to him."

"Oh? How's that?"

"Told him he had to show a profit in the next three months, or he'd never get General Manager," Joe said, settling back into his chair.

Beans's eyebrows rose, his beer bottle poised midway to his mouth. "You told him that?"

"Yup. About time that boy figured out the business or got on with his life. Can't have him hanging around the dealership losin' me money."

"Joe, have you ever thought that maybe he wasn't cut out for the car business?"

"Yeah." He sighed. "But he's my only son. If I can't leave the dealership to him, who else?"

"You could sell it and retire," Beans suggested. "We could get ourselves a boat, sit out in the Gulf, and fish for the rest of our days."

"I've thought of that, too, but I wanted to give the boy one last chance."

"So how long do you think he'll last before he figures out he's just not gonna cut it?" Beans asked.

Joe chuckled. "About two months."

"I'll bet ya a six-pack, he doesn't make it one." Beans tipped up the beer bottle, draining the last drops, and then belched his satisfaction.

"A six-pack? Let's not be cheap. I'll bet you an entire case of your favorite brew, he makes it two months before he throws in the towel." Joe adjusted the volume on the television and leaned forward. "Shhh. Here it comes."

"Stay tuned for the late news with Jenny Masters and Brian Frazier, brought to you by Peschke Motors."

"I can't believe I let him talk me into

this," Janine grumbled. Adjusting the straps tied around the back of her neck, she glanced at her image in the mirror of the ladies restroom at Peschke Motors. She had to admit the top of the miniscule jungle-woman costume looked great, fitting her breasts a bit tight, accentuating their fullness. The matching brown suede bottoms, a cross between short-shorts and a skirt, was another matter altogether. The thing barely covered her cheeks and was sure to give the cameraman an eyeful of her ass. So much for anyone taking her acting seriously.

Janine sighed. She'd fought a losing battle against her over-abundant curves ever since she'd "blossomed" at age twelve. Her life-long dream to become a serious actress appeared like an impossibility. At every audition, the casting directors couldn't see past her breasts to her acting ability. They wanted her to play in their beds, not act in their plays.

The few who'd bothered to audition her, as well as an acting coach she'd spent a summer studying under, had suggested she go for the vamp roles—and anything a Pamela Anderson-type might be considered for. Janine's confidence had been dented by their well-meaning advice, but she knew she was capable of more than blonde-bimbo performances. If her idol, Marilyn Monroe, could rise above her caricatured image to impress critics before her death, then Janine Davis could, too. Not that she was in a hurry to die to earn those accolades.

She'd prove everyone wrong—when she got enough money together to move out to Los Angeles. In the meantime, she was trying her luck in Austin, the newest cultural center frequented by famous actors from Hollywood. She hoped to be discovered while appearing in the local plays she'd been auditioning for, if she could actually convince a director to let her have one of the leading roles. But auditioning didn't pay the rent, and commercials were the closest thing to "real" acting as she could get right now and make a living.

Where was that Tanner Pesky, anyway? She was due in front of the cameras in less than five minutes, and there was no way in hell she was wearing this little, jungle-print handkerchief. She tugged at the bra of the itsy bitsy outfit in an attempt to cover as much of her chest as she could.

A knock on the door made her groan.

"It's time, Miss Davis," came a male voice, not Tanner's, through the hollow panel of the bathroom door.

"I'll be right out," she called. Alternating between tugging down the hem of the bottoms to cover her fanny, and pulling up the top to cover her breasts, she stormed out of the bathroom, across the showroom floor, and out into the lighted car lot.

Judging by the gauntlet of wolf calls she passed through to get to the television crew, every salesman in the dealership must have stayed late. They all wanted to witness the live filming by a group of college students Tanner hired to keep the budget low. As part of the crew's curriculum requirement, the commercial would air live on the university's public television station.

A man carrying a spider monkey approached and shoved the critter into her arms. "This is Spunky. You need to keep a hold on the monkey at all times, or he'll take off. Catching him will take us hours."

"Hey! Nobody said anything about a monkey." Janine pushed the little guy back at his handler, but the jerk turned and trotted to a position beyond the spotlights. Her chances of being taken seriously as an actress slipping through the seams of her skimpy costume and the busy fingers of the monkey, Janine suppressed the urge to scream.

"Quiet, everybody. Two minutes to take," the young director's voice boomed through a megaphone. "Where's Tanner?"

The animal handler called to Janine from the sidelines. "Remember, whatever you do, don't let go of the monkey."

"Right, don't let go of the monkey."

Janine's head swiveled side to side in search of the nutcase who'd talked her into this crazy commercial. She'd felt more in control on the bucking mechanical bull at the convention than she did right now.

Suddenly, the crowd of used car salesmen parted. Tanner strode toward her with his long, loose-limbed gait and all the confidence and charm of a professional actor. Tanner, dressed casually in his ever-present blue jeans, chambray shirt, cowboy hat and cowboy boots, smiled as he worked his way through the crowd of onlookers.

Janine snorted. *I'll bet he's never ridden a horse a day in his life.*

He walked right up and turned the full force of his smile on her.

Damn. Her knees went weak, complementing the butterflies in her stomach and the monkey fidgeting in her arms.

As the cameras moved into position, panic filled her. "You never told me what my lines were. What am I supposed to say?"

"Just stand over there and look beautiful. I'll do all the rest." He adjusted his hat with enough confidence for both of them. "And smile when I introduce you. That frown makes you look mean."

Janine opened her mouth to carve his enormous ego down to size and remind him she was an actress, not a model.

Before one word could cross Janine's lips, she was cut off by the cameraman. "Mr. Peschke, I hope you're ready because this is not a rehearsal, you're going live in five...four...three...two..." He pointed 'one'. The camera was trained on Tanner, the red button lit, and the feed was direct.

Without missing a beat, Tanner smiled, looking completely at ease in front of the camera. "Howdy, folks. It's a jungle out there. We know how difficult wading through the gimmicks and sales jargon is when buying a used car."

She had to admit he sounded charming and genuine. After sabotaging her job with BS-Squared, he'd conned Janine into taking this job. She bet he could sell ice to Eskimos.

Spunky's hairy little hand slipped beneath the bra of her outfit.

Janine slapped at his hand, eliciting a shriek from the monkey. "You must be a male," she muttered, wishing Tanner would fall on his pretty face in front of the camera.

"Are you sick of the new car prices and immediate depreciation when you drive a car off the lot? Let us take the monkey off your back..." Tanner swung an arm in her direction.

Spunky crawled up on her shoulders and played with her hair. *How about getting this monkey off my back?* Crap. She'd spent hours trying to fix her hair beautifully for the commercial. *Great, when they finally get the cameras on me, I look like the monkey.*

"...and show you what we've got in low mileage, pre-owned vehicles at rock-bottom prices."

At that moment, the creature latched onto the strings holding her halter-top in place. She felt her boobs dip and her stomach knotted.

"Stop that, Spunky," she whispered, making a grab for both of his tiny, dexterous fingers and the tail that seemed just as facile.

The monkey ignored her, chattering happily, hands and tail dodging her flailing attempts.

"Join us this weekend for our 'Monkey Off Your Back Sale.' We'll be servin' free banana milkshakes to all the folks who come out." Tanner's voice kept up the running monologue despite the monkey's antics, true to form for a car salesman.

Janine simmered as she struggled for control. *Let's get this over with before this monkey craps on me.*

Joe adjusted the volume on the set a little higher. "Not too bad, so far. A little dry, but gets the message across, don't you think?" He glanced at Beans for confirmation. All he got was a huge yawn and an exaggerated rolling of the eyes. "Well, it ain't over yet. Give him a chance, will ya?" Joe grumbled.

"Didn't say a word, Joe," Beans said, in his soft southern drawl.

"Ya didn't have to." Joe pressed his lips together.

"Let us take the monkey off your back." Tanner swept his hand to the right, and the camera took in a woman in a skimpy jungle costume with a monkey sitting on her shoulders. "Drop by this weekend and meet Spunky the Monkey and Janine who'll be celebrating the beginning of our Jungle Days of Summer sale-abration."

"Whoa, Beans, am I seein' what I'm seein'?" Joe scooted forward in his seat.

"I need my specs." Beans fumbled in his shirt pocket for his reading glasses and then hooked them over his ears. A moment later, he produced a long, low whistle and leaned forward himself. "By golly, maybe the boy's got something there."

"Not, something—someone," Joe corrected.

Edging closer to the screen, Beans squinted into his reading glasses. "What's that monkey tryin' to do to that girl?"

Joe scratched his head. "I don't know, but I think it's gettin' fresh with her...uh...tah-tahs."

"Yup, and them's some bodacious tah-

tahs, if you ask me." Beans's bushy eyebrows rose to the middle of his high forehead.

"Now, it's crawling around her neck. What's that Tanner's sayin'?" Joe turned his good ear toward the speaker.

Beans shrugged. "Who cares? I want to see what that monkey's gonna do next. Don't crowd the T.V."

Tanner looked a little distracted now, saying his lines and glancing worriedly over his shoulder at each ear-piercing shriek from the increasingly animated duo.

The monkey jerked the ties of the halter-top the girl wore and pulled them high above her head.

Joe's jaw dropped as the top loosened, exposing creamy skin, and the woman's eyes rounded, her mouth shaping into an "O" as Tanner dove between her and the camera. A high-pitched squeal sounded through the speakers, coming, no doubt, from the pretty blonde.

In the next second, the cause of the commotion, namely one hairy little monkey, leapt into view with a halter bra hanging from his nimble fingers.

Tanner stood in front of Janine, shielding her from the cameras that shifted to the right then the left, trying to get a better view of what was going on with the topless beauty.

Joe's mouth hung open for a few

moments, and then he broke into a delighted grin. He clapped Beans on the back and chuckled. "I think you're right. The boy's got something there. Care to up the ante on our bet? I think two months may be sellin' the boy short."

Beans scratched his chin, his lips twitching. "Could be, could be."

"What say, you and me make a surprise visit to the lot tomorrow?"

"Wouldn't miss it for the world." Beans settled back into his chair. "I want to meet that monkey—and the girl, of course."

Chapter Three

Peschke Motors had never seen a turnout for a sales event like the one for the "Jungle Days of Summer."

"Don't you think it's time to call in the big dog?" Scott Greenblatt, the assistant sales manager, asked, worry thick in his words.

Tanner stood with Scott atop the steps of the showroom building and watched the quickly filling parking lot with satisfaction. "Dad and Beans had plans to go fishin' today. He left me in charge." He winked at Scott and added, "Besides, won't it be more fun to slide the sales report on his desk on Monday and watch his eyes pop out?"

Scott laughed half-heartedly. "That's if we manage to close a deal with all this hoopla goin' on."

"Not to worry. It's all under control. I called in all the sales staff who were scheduled off and offered everyone commission and a half for any deals closed by the end of today."

"Commission and a half? That might set a fire under their butts, alright. Whooee! Ain't your Daddy gonna be surprised?"

Tanner rubbed his hands together. "That's the plan."

Scott aimed a sharp blue gaze at Tanner.

"What I wanna know is how you talked Janine into comin' back today after last night's excitement?"

"Janine's a professional." Tanner made the statement with a straight face, smiling inwardly.

"Son, you've got a gift. As mad as that little lady was last night, I'd a thought she'd sooner poke you in the eye than come back here."

Tanner winced, remembering his last conversation with the lady in question. She'd been ready to filet him after Spunky the Monkey had exposed her in public.

Her exact words had been, "You'd better get me something to wear, *right now*, or I'll personally cut off your balls and feed them to that monkey." She managed that while pressing her plump breasts to his back, shielding herself from eager eyes and shifting cameras.

Tanner wasn't too sure the live feed had been cut at that point. For the sake of his jewels, he hoped Janine never found out otherwise. The woman had a real mean streak for someone who looked as soft and sweet as cotton candy.

He shuffled with her all the way to the ladies room, then run to find her a spare mechanic's shirt.

Janine snatched the shirt through the

door of the women's bathroom, slamming the door on his fingers.

"Ow!" He cradled his hurt fingers and silently screamed every curse word he knew. "That hurt!"

"Serves you right, you no good car salesman."

Exasperated, Tanner leaned his forehead against the door and tried for a gentler approach. "Ah come on, Janine. It wasn't my fault the monkey was a little fresh."

"A little?" Her voice rose to a shriek.

"Okay, so he really did a number on you, but I need you here tomorrow. You can't let me down," he pleaded.

"I will not co-star with that smelly little lecher."

"But the whole world is expectin' you and the monkey at the sale this weekend." When she didn't respond, he let his temper get the best of him. "I can sue for breach of contract, you know."

"Sue? Ha! See how much I care. I quit."

His mind raced. "I'll give you lines to say in the next commercial."

The door cracked an inch and one deep blue eye peered through. "Lines I write myself?"

Lowering his face to look her in the eye, he promised, "Yes, anything. Just say you'll stay."

The eye narrowed, and he held his breath while she thought about his offer.

"No." The door slammed shut. "I can't even show my face in public after last night. I'll have to dye my hair and change my stage name."

"Your name's not Janine?"he asked, disappointed because he thought it suited her just fine.

"Of course it is! But I can't use it now."

"If it's the money, I'll double your fee." Tanner cringed as he said that. *There goes the profit line.*

"You don't get it, Mr. Moneybags. The issue is not the money. It's the embarrassment."

Tanner opened his mouth, then shut it and thought for a moment. Up to this point, he'd been talking about what *he* needed. What would a good salesman do when faced with a tough customer?

Taking a different tack, he launched into a new assault. "Do you think Marilyn Monroe or Meryl Streep would have given up after a little embarrassment?" No response. "Don't you think they had their share of mishaps and failures at the beginning of their acting careers?" He held his breath for her reply.

"I suppose so," had been her tentative response.

Encouraged, he'd continued, "Did that

stop them?"

"No...but I'm sure they weren't stripped by a monkey on prime time."

Okay for her to still be mad—at least she was listening. "Maybe not, but I'd bet my last dollar they had their share of humiliations. That didn't stop them from makin' it big. Did it?"

"No, I guess not," she replied reluctantly.

"You know why, don't you?" He waited. If she didn't take the bait, he was sunk.

"Why?"

He had her wiggling on the hook. Now, all he had to do was reel her in. "Because they persevered. They put their acting first. They would have gotten right back out there, heads held high. So, Janine, if you're feelin' humiliated—*act* like you're not."

"What do you mean?"

"Tomorrow during the sale, *act* like it was all planned." Silence again. Had he pushed her too far? He hoped not. Janine was the best idea he'd had so far as Peschke Motors was concerned. She had to stay in order for his campaign to work. "Your performance could be the best actin' you've ever done if you can make the audience believe you weren't the slightest bit affected by what happened."

A very unladylike snort sounded through the door. "You got that straight."

"So, what do you say?"

"Double the fee?" Her voice strengthened.

"You got it." *Even if I have to pay for it out of my own pocket.*

"I write my own lines?"

He mentally winced and determined he would cross that bridge when it appeared. "You got it."

She groaned, the sound muffled like she was pressed against the door. "I don't know."

"Come on, Janine. Think of this as the first rung in the ladder to your acting career."

He heard a loud sigh. "Well...okay." When she'd opened the door, he saw her expression was still a little sullen. "For the sake of my career—not for you."

"That's my girl." He pulled her into his arms and hugged her close. With his arm still draped around her shoulder, he led her out into the deserted showroom. She looked awfully cute in the shirt he'd given her to wear. It was long and hung to mid-thigh, completely covering her little jungle skirt, giving the impression the shirt was all she had on. And it almost was. The monkey had refused to part with the bra. Fortunately, Spunky had returned to his handler, carrying his trophy.

Squeezing her close again, Tanner leaned over and kissed her forehead. "Thanks for stickin' with me, Janine. You're a real trouper." Then he walked her to her car, wondering if it was too soon to ask her out for coffee, maybe dinner. Instead, she'd driven off and Tanner had returned to his apartment for a very cold shower.

"So, whatcha gonna do about all the reporters settin' up in the showroom?"

Scott's question brought Tanner back to his present dilemma. Janine didn't know about the news crews that had started calling for interviews before the store even opened.

"I've got that handled, too," he lied.

"Did you know some of the reporters are from as far away as Houston and Dallas?"

"Yeah. It's all sensational advertising, and Dad doesn't have to pay a cent." Satisfaction puffed out his chest. Sure, his Dad would be over the moon, but Janine Davis was going to give him fits. One thing for her to be humiliated on local television, but the response meant the whole state of Texas wanted in on the story.

Scott glanced around the showroom. "So where is Janine?"

"Don't know, haven't seen her yet." Tanner glanced at his watch. "If you'll excuse me, I'd better see what's keepin' her." He smiled and clapped his hand against the older man's shoulder, before pushing his way through the crush of people to enter the showroom.

"Hey, Tanner, loved the commercial last night," called Rudy, one of the dealership's best salesmen.

"Thanks, Rudy."

"So what's next? Last night will be a tough act to follow."

He grinned. "Yeah, I know what you mean. I was thinkin' of maybe buildin' on the jungle theme and incorporating different animals in each commercial."

"Sounds good, as long as you have the blonde with them. She's what made the commercial last night."

"Yeah, I agree. I'm in the process of negotiating with her to stay with the commercials throughout the summer, longer if possible. I think she's got something."

"I'd say she's got a couple of somethings." Rudy winked.

Tanner's smile froze and his chest tightened. He couldn't blame Rudy for pointing out the obvious, but Janine wasn't Rudy's find, she was Tanner's. And he didn't like the crude comments from the salesman. This time, he'd let it pass. Nothing could spoil this day. A lot rode on his success. "Speakin' of Janine, where is she?"

"She's back in the women's restroom." Rudy hooked a thumb over his shoulder. "The animal handler's back there, too. You might want to see what's keepin' them. She's been in there a long time."

Tanner squared his shoulders, ready for battle with the lovely Janine and looking forward to every minute. "Yeah, I'm on my way."

As he strode to the office area where the restrooms were located, he could hear the commotion before he actually saw it.

"Miss Davis, please come out of there. Everyone's come to see you and Spunky." The handler stood in the exact same place Tanner had been the evening before, pleading with her from outside the restroom door.

Tanner shook his head. *Men have no pride when it comes to a gorgeous woman.*

"I don't care. I'm not coming out," Janine said from behind the door. "And you can take away that hairy little psychopath."

"Look, Janine, honey. I don't know what got into him last night, but he's a perfect angel today. He's not going to give you any problems. Promise."

Tanner tapped the handler on the shoulder. "Hey, Tommy. What's the problem?"

The handler's face relaxed on a wave of relief. "I don't know. Stage fright, maybe?"

"Let me handle this. Go on into my office and wait there." Tanner steered him into an office a few doors down. When he turned back to the restroom, he took a deep breath to cool his irritation. "Janine, it's Tanner. Are you ready?"

"No. You can't be serious about me wearing the same costume as yesterday after what happened? It's covered in monkey slobber."

"Tommy promises Spunky will behave today. It won't happen again. You just need to tie the straps into knots and the monkey won't be able to untie it."

"This thing might as well be sprayed on as it is. I won't be able to get it off."

"I'll help you get it unknotted when the day's over." Tanner grinned, waiting for her indignant response . He wasn't disappointed.

"Oh, I'm sure you will." She huffed. "And that's supposed to make me feel safer?"

Tanner's smile widened. He was figuring out what got Janine fired up. "I'll find a saleswoman to help you, then. Now, are you gonna come out and behave like the professional you claim to be, or are you gonna stay in there and hide?"

That shut her up, and she opened the door cautiously. "Are you sure this is going to help my career?"

"Guarantee it," he whispered, caught by the worry in her pretty eyes.

"Sure, and I'm supposed to believe those words from a used car salesman?" She straightened, tossing her hair over shoulders.

"You know, I'm almost absolutely positive I don't even like animals. I only have to play with the monkey today, right?"

Tanner wanted more than anything to slide his lips across her forehead to wipe away the fine frown lines. But then he might be tempted to drop lower and smooth across her pouting lips. Instinctively, he knew a kiss wouldn't be nearly enough to satisfy him. With a camera crew awaiting their arrival, he couldn't afford to show up with a hard on.

The little Jungle-Jane outfit she wore looked even more revealing in the light of day. Did the woman have any idea how perfectly made her body was? Staring wasn't helping stifle his arousal. When he glanced up, he spotted a militant gleam sparkling in Janine's eyes.

Tanner pasted on a cheery smile. "All you have to do is hold Spunky and say the lines you wrote. Are you ready to face your fans?"

At that statement, her face perked up. "Fans? You mean there's someone here to see me?"

Glad there was no need to bluff, Tanner grinned. "Honey, there's a lot of someones here to see you."

Her smile dropped into a pretty worried frown. "Oh God, I'm not sure that's a good thing."

"Hey, at least your face is out there." He

bent his elbow and held it out in her direction. "Like I told you, this could be the beginning of something big."

Janine curled her hand into the crook of his arm. "All right, I'm sold. Lead the way, salesman."

After collecting Spunky, they walked down the corridor and into the crowded showroom. Janine's fingers pinched the inside of his arm. "You could have warned me the media was here," she said, from behind a tight smile.

He aimed a grin at the crowd and leaned toward her. "Would you have come out of the ladies room if I'd told you?"

She gave him a sideways glare that didn't dim the brilliance of her smile. "You are a very, very sneaky man, Tanner Pesky."

"It's Peschke, 'pesh-key'. Be sure to get it right for the reporters, honey."

"Yeah, Pesky. That's what I said."

He groaned and rolled his eyes. *Now, I find out she has a speech impediment—and I promised her lines.*

"Miss Davis. Mr. Peschke. Miss Davis." The reporters converged on them, shouting questions all at once.

Spunky let out a screech of panic and jumped from Janine's arms onto her shoulders.

Tanner felt Janine's hand tighten into a

death grip on his arm. Her smile appeared frozen and he saw the beginnings of panic rising in her eyes.

Raising a hand for silence, Tanner spoke loudly, "Please, folks. Let's back up. Spunky's gettin' a little excited by all the commotion. And the name's Tanner. Just Tanner." Then he gave them his most charming smile. "And this lovely lady is Janine—Janine Davis."

In the quiet that followed, he pulled Spunky from Janine's shoulders and deposited him back into her arms. He stared down at Janine, refusing to look away until he had her full attention. Then he winked.

Eyes widening a fraction, she responded with a genuine smile of pleasure at the same time as cameras flashed.

Tanner turned to the reporters. "We'll answer your questions before Janine and Spunky go out to greet the folks who've come here to meet them today." He pointed to a reporter. "Sir, what's your question?"

"My question is for you, Tanner."

He nodded. "Shoot."

"How'd you talk Janine into coming back after the monkey's antics last night? Janine seemed to have a few choice things to say. Not that any of them were printable." The crowd laughed.

Despite the corkscrew pinch Janine gave to his arm, Tanner managed a deep chuckle.

Janine had used a few words that would make a sailor blush. And she'd been so cute saying them.

"That was live?" she hissed next to his ear.

He leaned close and spoke through his teeth without moving his lips. "Smile, sweetheart. Remember, all part of the plan." To the reporter, he brandished his most professional smile. "Janine's a professional actress." That was for Janine. Hopefully, the plug would appease her. "She understands not everything goes according to the script."

"Yeah, but losing your top on public television is a little more humiliating than forgetting your lines," said another reporter, female this time. "How did she feel about that?"

"As I said, Janine is a professional actress, and she took the events all in stride."

The next questions were for Janine. Pride swelled Tanner's chest as she fielded every question, even the lewd and outrageous ones that left him scowling and ready to break heads. All the while, she charmed her audience with the breathy, girlish quality of her voice and the artless posing of her voluptuous figure.

Relief unwound the knot in his shoulders. She really was good at this. Maybe she wasn't Meryl Streep, but she was great in front of a camera. He knew instinctively her platinum hair and cream-colored skin would photograph well. The glossy red color of her lipstick and the tiny black mole beside her lips added a dramatic splash of color against an otherwise cream and gold canvas.

Tanner caught a glimpse of movement through the glass windows of the showroom floor. He searched the crowd of onlookers, his chest tightening when he spied his father and Beans wearing sunglasses and fishing hats in a ridiculous attempt to blend into the crowd. Great. Dad was here to make sure he didn't screw up things.

Just when Tanner thought the situation couldn't get worse, he saw another nightmare pushing her way through the crowd of people at the side door, waving for his attention. Barbara Stockton smiled and waved at him as if he was a long-lost lover. He had yet to tell his father about the botched deal, and he wouldn't tell him today—not if he could help it.

"Look everyone," he said, flashing a smile, "you're welcome to stay for refreshments, or join the folks who're shopping for a vehicle. Janine and I'll be minglin' with customers throughout the day."

Tanner left Janine surrounded by admirers and ducked out the front door, heading for safety among the customers jammed into the parking lot.

"Tanner, darling."

Barbara Stockton's drawl stopped him in his tracks. How had she managed to move through the crowd so quickly?

She hooked her arm in his and squeezed. "I've been meaning to talk to you since you left in such a hurry from the convention the other day."

His lips formed a thin line. "You kicked me out." He kept sight of his father as the older woman leaned close.

Joe Peschke frowned. The man probably thought Tanner was talking to one of Aggie Smithson's relatives. Irritated at her timing, but wanting a second shot at the deal, Tanner gritted his teeth and smiled at Barbara. "But I can't think of a lovelier woman who's ever left her heel marks on my behind."

She laughed silkily. "I'm not taking you away from anything, am I?" She glanced at Janine who was still surrounded by reporters.

"Janine? She's...hired help." He cringed inwardly at using Barbara's own words and for the next words he would say. "She's nothing more than arm candy, really. Now, you're what I call a real woman."

Touching a hand to her hair, she practically glowed. "Do you really think so?"

"But of course," he said smoothly. "Now, what brought you all the way over here? I thought our deal was off."

With a pretty moue of her lips, she replied, "I came to apologize for my behavior the other day, and to see if you're still interested in purchasing my old fleet."

"I don't know, Barbara. After more consideration, I'm not sure I can move that many pink cars," Tanner hedged. He couldn't believe he'd actually said that. Here was his chance to redeem the deal and he was telling Barbara he wasn't interested. Had he lost his mind?

Her finger trailed down the front of his shirt. "Ah, come on, Tanner honey. Tell me how I can sweeten the deal." Her tongue snaked out, traveling around bright red-painted lips.

Tanner widened his stance. Somewhere between the raging mechanical bull and Spunky's high-jinks, the tables had turned. He wasn't the supplicant here. "I'm not sure I can give you the price we originally agreed on…before you had me thrown out of the hotel the other day."

"Then, let's talk, darling." She'd moved in so close she was practically draped across his chest. Brushing her lips across his earlobe, she purred, "What's the right price?"

Adrenaline winged through his system. This was it. This was the chance he'd been waiting for to redeem himself in his father's eyes, to take charge of his standing in the used car business, and to prove he wasn't a complete failure when dealing with women. Excitement tinged with caution drove him to stand taller and hope he wasn't being a complete idiot as he answered the woman's question. "Twenty thousand less than the original deal." As the words left his mouth, he glanced across the lot to where his father stood. For a full five seconds, Tanner held his breath, waiting for Barbara's response, certain he'd blown his second chance.

"Oh, honey, you've...got a deal," She backed away far enough to offer her hand to seal the deal.

Tanner let the trapped air out of his lungs, producing a wash of relief so profound his knees weakened.

Barbara brushed her hands together. "Well, now that that's done..." BS-Squared's fingers curled around his arm, her nails biting into him. "Do you mind if I have a word with Janine while I'm here?"

"No, of course I don't mind. She's a free agent." Tanner's bullshit meter jerked into the red by Barbara's sudden change of subject and demeanor. "May I ask why?"

Barbara let go of Tanner's arm, a smile curling her blood-red lips. "I want to offer her a job."

Tanner's stomach completed a full gainer

and he blurted out, "I'm sorry, but she's working for me through the summer."

The beauty maven's professionally arched brows rose. "Do you have a contract?"

"Well, it's under revision..." Revision, hell. Tanner hadn't even considered a contract. He'd never hired an actress before Janine. What kind of contract did actresses need?

Barbara's fingernail scraped across Tanner's shoulder in a long, slow slide. Her lips puffed out all sultry-like, reminding Tanner of when he'd been inside her hotel suite being sized up as the next meat course on her table. "I feel badly about firing her last weekend, and I want to make it up to her."

Tanner stepped away from the woman, his eyes narrowing. "She's not interested."

"Why don't we let her decide?" Barbara insisted.

"I promise you, Janine is not interested." Tanner held back his anger and panic. Janine was turning out to be a gold mine, and he didn't want anyone else staking a claim on her...talents.

"I'm not interested in what?" The object of his panic walked up behind him with the monkey in her arms.

"In coming back to work for me," Barbara announced, a sweet-as-sugar smile on her lips.

"Oh, I'm not interested, am I?" Janine's voice dipped dangerously low.

Tanner recognized the first signs of the thundercloud building in Janine's eyes. "I thought after the way you were treated last weekend I could safely say you weren't interested in working for Mrs. Stockton again."

"And you think I like working with a nasty monkey any better?" She glanced down at the animal wrapped around her arm. "No offense, Spunky."

"I can guarantee we never use monkeys in any advertising for Barbara Stockton Beauty Secrets," Barbara interjected.

"But Janine," Tanner cajoled, "...the monkey's not so bad. He made the commercial last night." As soon as the words were out of his mouth, Tanner wished he could take them back, but knew they'd come with her footprints.

"So the monkey was the commercial, was he?" Gathering the little leash, she peeled the monkey from her arm and handed him to Tanner. "Here, you like him so much—you hold him." To the monkey, she said, "Sorry, Spunky. It's been fun."

"Now Janine, be reasonable."

Spunky obviously didn't like the change either, because he scrambled from Tanner's arms to his shoulders and knocked away his cowboy hat. Giving an ear-piercing scream, the little monkey bounced on his back legs while keeping a death grip in Tanner's hair.

Pain attacked his skull with each of Spunky's bounces. Desperate, Tanner reached out his empty hand. "Honey, you know I didn't mean it the way it sounded. Take back the monkey, please. He likes you better."

"No way. He was your idea—you deal with him." The blonde turned to Barbara. "What kind of terms are you offering me?"

"Janine, you can't be serious." Tanner hurried to her side, while the monkey pounded the top of his head like a bongo drum. "Hey, cut that out, Spunky. Tommy, where the hell are you?"

Ignoring his predicament, Janine continued her conversation with Barbara. "I'd want double the salary with a signed contract and a specified appearance schedule."

"You've got it," Barbara agreed immediately.

"Janine…" Tanner stepped between the two women, hoping to stop the handshake that would seal the deal.

The sudden movement startled Spunky, and he leapt onto Barbara's head, then across to a light pole behind the startled woman.

"Oh no, Spunky!" Janine yelled, the handshake forgotten as she rushed to pole. "The handler said not to let him go. He's almost impossible to catch."

Tanner glanced up at the monkey scaling the light pole, silently thanking the critter for his perfect timing. "That's okay, he'll come down sooner or later."

"You don't understand. If he gets up into the electrical lines, he'll be killed." Janine glanced up the pole at the monkey, then back to Tanner, her big, blue, beautiful eyes, clouded with worry. "Please, get him down, Tanner."

Tanner's chest tightened. How could he walk away from such a heartfelt plea? Afraid her next step would be to turn on the waterworks, Tanner heaved a sigh and looked up the pole at the delighted monkey.

The creature had climbed up to perch on the banner strung from the pole to the top of the showroom building, advertising the "Monkey Off Your Back" sale. The irony did not escape the media, and they rushed outside to film the little monkey's antics.

Scotty walked up behind Tanner. "You weren't supposed to let go of the monkey," he said, his tone dry.

"I know that, damn it. Get maintenance on the radio and have them bring me a ladder, ASAP."

Scott clicked the button on his walkie-talkie. A maintenance truck arrived in minutes with the requested ladder.

Reassuring himself that everything was going to be all right, Tanner reminded himself the monkey wouldn't be up there if not for his negligence. The least he could do was go get the little guy before he got injured. It didn't hurt a bit that reporters kept clicking cameras all around as well. This whole new fiasco was yet another opportunity to get more airtime.

When the maintenance man set the ladder in place, Tanner made the climb himself. He figured the effort wouldn't be much to snag the monkey as long as the ladder was tall enough—which it was...just. Standing on the top rung, his arm hugging the round pole, he grabbed for the monkey.

Spunky moved a little farther out on the banner.

"Come here, Spunky," he said, doing his utmost to keep his irritation with the miniature primate out of his voice. "I have a nice banana waiting for you at the bottom if you'll just come here."

Spunky moved out a little more and eyed the far end of the banner.

If he wanted to grab the monkey, Tanner knew it was now or never. Failure was not an option with Janine, his dad, and the entire state of Texas watching. He had to go for the monkey.

Making a jabbing stretch, Tanner grabbed

for the monkey, but Spunky was quicker and skittered away across the top of the banner. Tanner in mid-reach, his fingers clawing the air, felt the ladder listing to the right. Letting out a startled yelp, he grabbed for the banner and hung tight as the ladder rocked once, then fell crashing to the ground.

Just as he was congratulating himself on his luck that the banner was strong enough to hold his weight, the monkey swung out to join him.

"You sorry little..."

A renting sound ripped through the air, announcing the demise of the banner and the loss of Tanner's precarious perch. The end attached to the light pole tore free, carrying Tanner in a mad swing toward the showroom steps. Tanner yelled long and loud as he swung through the air toward certain pain. Putting out his feet, he managed to break his crash, absorbing the force of the fall with bent knees.

Tanner heard an excited shriek and stared upwards just as the monkey slid down the ruined banner and landed in his arms.

"Sweet Jesus! Did you see that Beans?" Joe's voice rose above the stunned silence.

One person in the crowd clapped, another joined him, then another, until the applause grew louder, joined by cheers from the people gathering around the showroom steps.

Three feet away, Janine stood tall in her jungle outfit, one hand planted on a hip, a grin stretched across her face. Raising her voice enough to carry over the noise from the crowd, she shouted, "Way to go, Tarzan."

Chapter Four

"It's practically ungodly to have auditions this early in the morning, don't you think, Janine?"

Smiling though nervous, Janine shook her head at her friend, Kelly Shannon. "Nine o'clock for most normal people is halfway through the morning."

They stood in line outside the theater in downtown Austin, awaiting their turn to audition for the latest Hal Miller play. Janine scanned through the sheets of script that had just been handed down the line, trying to get a feel for the characters and the general mood of the story line.

Tryouts hadn't begun yet, but the line kept growing, the closer it got to nine o'clock. Her stomach gurgled loudly. Maybe she should have skipped breakfast. The last thing she needed was to lose her breakfast before an audience. She smoothed a sweaty palm down the side of her skirt and breathed deep breaths to calm herself.

"Oh my God! It's you," cried one of the latecomers, glancing down at the newspaper she held. "Aren't you Janine Davis?"

Heat burned Janine's cheeks as the other woman gushed. "Yes, I'm Janine Davis. But how did you know that?"

"Girlfriend, you're practically a celebrity." The stranger slid a section of the newspaper under Janine's nose, jabbing a finger at the photograph on the first page. "You're Janine of the Tarzan and Janine phenom."

I'm a phenom? Her back stiffened. Janine scanned the picture, butterflies turning cartwheels in her belly. On the front page of the section of paper the woman held up was a picture of Janine in her skimpy jungle outfit, reaching up for Spunky the Monkey as Tanner held onto the banner in mid-swing. The caption read, "Tarzan and Janine Swing Into Action." And it was the entertainment section. *What a freaking nightmare!*

"Oh, my God! Janine, this is wonderful!" Kelly snatched the paper from the woman to scan the photograph and headline. "Think of all the promo you can get with this. It could be the launch of your career, the break you've been waiting for. This is utterly fab!"

Hesitant to get all excited about a photograph depicting a disaster the size of the Titanic, or maybe one of its dinghies, Janine couldn't help but smile at Kelly's enthusiasm. "I guess the publicity couldn't hurt anything, huh?" Her smile waned. "You don't think it'll hurt my chances of getting this part, do you?"

"Hurt your chances?" Kelly's smile stretched wide. "The director won't forget your face even if a hundred girls try out. You've got this audition nailed."

Janine's brow wrinkled, her many rejections making her hesitant to actually hope. "You really think so?"

"All you have to do is get the lines right, and you're home free."

Janine's fading smile twisted into a grimace. "All I have to do is get the lines right," she muttered, breaking out in a sweat at the thought. "Kelly, let me read these through one more time, please."

Kelly gave her shoulder a hug. "You'll have them memorized by the time they open this door."

"I can't afford to blow this chance," she said. "I've worked so hard to get to this point." All the years of acting lessons and bit parts in plays should have amounted to something.

Kelly raised her pages. "Go ahead, shoot."

Clearing her throat, Janine began, "Here's your wine, William. Now perhaps we can discuss the *debacle at Deb's Diner*." Good Lord, what a tongue twister!

Kelly cleared her throat, filling in for William. "Why Linda, what debacle are you referring to?"

"You know perfectly well." Janine turned away from Kelly like the script indicated.

"What was I to think when you left during lunch, without a word or a clue?"

The door to the theater opened, interrupting Janine's mini-rehearsal, sending butterflies in full force to invade her stomach.

A pasty-faced young man held the door. "Mr. Miller's ready to begin auditions for Linda. Who's first?"

"That would be me." Janine raised her hand, battling the panic attack making her heart race and her vision blur.

"Well, come on," he said impatiently then turned, entering the building without looking back.

Janine dove for the door, jamming her hand through the crack before it closed and locked. Once inside, she ran to keep up with the man.

Backstage was dark, with only the lights from center stage providing enough illumination for them to avoid tripping over boxes and wires. Too soon, they stood at the edge of the curtain. Janine fought the urge to grab the assistant's sleeve to stop him.

The assistant halted and turned. "What's your name, again?"

"Never said. J-J-Janine." She stuttered, cleared her throat, and tried again. "Janine Davis." There, that wasn't so bad.

The assistant stepped out onto the stage. "Mr. Miller, the first actor is Ms. Janine

Davis." He turned toward her, blinking when he realized she hadn't followed him onstage. A frown marked his brow and he gave her a beckoning wave.

Jerking into the light, Janine hurried across the stage and peered into the dark cavern of the theater, stage lights blinding her vision.

A disembodied voice shouted above the thundering beat of her pulse in her eardrums. "Ms. Davis, please read Linda's first line in Act II, Scene 1. My assistant will read William's lines."

"Yes, sir." She opened her script to the beginning of the act, her hands shaking as she clutched the pages high enough to read. After a deep, calming breath, she began. "Here's your wine, William." Handing an imaginary glass of wine to the assistant, Janine congratulated herself on a smooth first line. She hoped the butterflies in her stomach didn't manifest themselves into upchucked bagel and orange juice before she got out her next line. "Now perhaps we can discuss *Simon and Garfunkel while Deb does Dallas.*"

The assistant's head jerked up, eyes wide. Then he shouted with laughter, clutching at his sides.

Horrified, Janine darted a glance toward where the director sat before aiming a glare at his crazy assistant. "Why are you laughing?"

she asked out of the side of her mouth, before again aiming a smile toward the lights.

"What you said..." The assistant snorted, pressed a hand into his side, and gasped for air. "Are you for real?"

Janine's brows slammed together. "Of course, I'm for real. And please stop," she whispered harshly. "What will Mr. Miller think?"

"Who cares? After you butchered that last line, it won't matter."

"I don't understand." Dread took the place of confusion. "What did I say that you find so damn funny?"

"Ms. Davis," the voice from beyond the footlights boomed. "To put it politely, you didn't say the lines quite as written."

"I didn't?" Janine swallowed hard on the lump forming in her throat. Dear God, she hoped this was all some big joke between the director and his assistant. She'd read the lines *exactly* as written. She wanted this part. Needed it. Winning the lead in a Hal Miller play launched serious acting careers. And she'd had enough of brainless beer and car commercials.

"No, you didn't," said the faceless Mr. Miller. "Next."

The assistant hooked Janine's elbow and tugged her toward the other end of the stage.

Janine dug her heels into the hardwood

flooring. "Does this mean I got the part?"

The assistant shook his head. "Not today, honey." His fingers tightened around Janine's arm.

She shook free of his hand and faced the theater and the faceless Mr. Miller. "May I ask why I'm not getting the part?"

"No, but I'll answer anyway," he said, his words sounding snipped. "You're simply not right."

"Is it may hair?" she asked, lifting a hand to push her hair behind her ears. "I can cut it or die it. You name the color."

"No, no, Ms. Davis. Your hair is fine. It's *not* the hair."

"Is it my voice? I can speak lower, if you like," she said, lowering her voice to an unnatural alto.

A cough sounded. "I promise it's not your voice. I want someone less...*flamboyant*," he said.

"Is it because of the Pesky Motors commercial?" She hated the desperation in her voice, but couldn't stand by and do nothing while her dream slipped through her fingers. "I won't do any more of the commercials if that will help?"

"Oh no, I think you should continue to do them. Apparently, you've found your niche. *Stick to it.* Now, you've taken enough of my time, Ms. Davis. George, bring in the next actress, please."

George cleared his throat beside her. His head tilted toward the stage door.

With humiliation burning her cheeks, Janine lifted her chin, squared her shoulders, and swept off the stage. She made it all the way to her car before she broke down and had a good cry. Somehow, all this was Tanner Pesky's fault, she just knew it.

* * *

"Tanner, old buddy." Rip O'Rourke's voice blasted through the phone receiver into Tanner's ear. "I've got Gage and Jesse on conference call with me. We wanted to congratulate you on your commercials' overwhelming success."

Tanner scrubbed a hand through his hair. "You're kiddin' me, right?" He'd been up all night thinking through the fiasco of the live commercial and his swing into infamy the day before.

"Damnedest thing I've ever seen," Gage's voice piped in.

"I know, I almost spewed beer on my television screen when the monkey stole the girl's top." Jesse chuckled. "I'm thinking of hirin' you and Janine to do all the commercials for my ranch supply chain. Should give us a huge boost in sales."

"What did your dad think?" Gage asked, his voice casual.

Tanner sighed. "I haven't talked to him yet." He and Beans had snuck away after the press surrounded him.

"If he even has a spark of humor, the man'll love what you did." Jesse whistled. "And the banner swingin' was over the top. Brilliant, if you ask me. All the Austin news programs were coverin' it. What a coup for free advertising."

"Thanks." Tanner didn't know what else to say.

"We want to know where you found the babe." Rip cleared his throat. "And is she married?"

"Can I get her number?" Gage asked.

Tanner's teeth clenched. "I met Janine at the hotel after my meeting with Barbara Stockton."

"Oh yeah?" Jesse snorted. "How come you didn't mention her when you were tellin' us how the deal went sour?"

He'd told them about the failed deal and how he'd botched it, leaving out the embarrassing particulars relating to the mechanical bull.

"Buddy, you've been holdin' out on us." Rip laughed. "Can't blame you though. That Janine is one hot hoochie-mamma."

Anger spiked through his veins. "She's not a hoochie-mamma, she's a bonafide actress."

"Emphasis on boner." Rip laughed at his own joke.

Tanner's jaw sagged and he held the phone away to glare at it. "Is that all you guys called about?"

"Yeah, we thought we'd cheer you up. The commercials are all the buzz."

Trust Gage to bring the conversation back to what was relevant. Tanner's irritation eased a bit.

"Be proud, dude."

"I still want the babe's number," Rip said.

"Not gettin' it." Tanner's jaw clenched.

"Let us know when the next episode of The Tarzan and Janine Show airs," Jesse added. "Might have to call a meeting of the TBC at the local sports bar to watch it together."

"Keep up the great work," Gage added. "Later, man."

Tanner hung up the phone and yelled, "Scott, tell Jill that if my dad calls, I'm not available. Tell him I'm out on the lot or something."

Scott stepped in, with a wicked grin. "What's the matter, Tarzan, Janine got your loin cloth in a wad?"

"Fuck you." Tanner buried his head in his hands. "I can't believe they caught all that on T.V." He glanced up at Scott. "Now no one in Austin'll take me seriously. How am I to make it in this business, much less show a profit in three months?"

"What a baby. Cheer up, Tanner, and read this." Scott tossed the morning paper into the middle of his desk.

Tanner gave him a baleful stare. "Good God, it's even in the paper?"

"Yeah, flip to the entertainment section. You'll find yourself in all your glory." Scott chuckled. "Not a bad picture of you and Janine."

"You're enjoyin' this way too much," Tanner grumbled, flipping through the paper. "The entertainment section? They could have at least put it on the front page, or the business page or even the sports section."

"Why are you complainin'? I see it as free advertising. You should be thankful, instead of grousing about being humiliated in front of the entire city of Austin."

Tanner glared at Scott. "Thanks, I feel much better."

He turned his attention to the newsprint and the story on the front page of the entertainment section. The photo was of him swinging from the banner with the monkey sliding down behind him. The picture filled half the page, giving him a surge of hope. "Wow, that *is* good advertising. Look, you can even read Peschke Motors on the banner."

"See, I told you to cheer up. It was a

great stunt, if you ask me. You couldn't have pulled it off any better if you'd planned it."

"Which I didn't," Tanner muttered.

"Point is, the advertising is great and the public loved it. The phones have been ringin' off the hook from all the media folks in the city. They want to know when they can expect the next episode of The Tarzan and Janine Show."

His buddies in the TCB had said the same thing. Tanner cringed. "That's a question I'd like to know myself."

"What do you mean?"

"I don't have Janine under contract. She may not agree to do another commercial. Not only that, I've got competition now."

"What, is the circus in town?" Scott's shoulders jerked with suppressed laughter.

Tanner gave him a blistering glare. "No. Old BS-Squared offered her a job and Janine didn't refuse it. In all the ruckus, I didn't get to her in time to firm up our deal."

"Did she take the job with Ms. Stockton?"

"Not exactly." Tanner blew out a deep gust of air. Did he really stand a chance against the beauty products maven?

"What do you mean, not exactly?"

"Just that, Janine didn't say yes or no. She said she'd think about it." Tanner's desk phone buzzed and he jabbed a finger at the intercom.

" I told you not to disturb me."

"No, you didn't, and your father's on line two, Mr. Peschke," came the calm voice of Jill, the receptionist.

"But I don't want to talk—"

"Tanner, is that you boy?" Joe Peschke's voice boomed over the intercom.

The *boy* in question leaned back in his chair and pressed his fingers to the bridge of his nose, his eyes squeezing shut, trying to block out the nightmare that was his life. "Yes, sir, it's me," he answered, schooling his voice to flat and emotionless. Might as well get the lecture over with. Dad would go on about how inadequate he was at this business and Tanner would promise to try harder.

He really should tell his dad about his billions, then the old man wouldn't look at him as such a failure. But how would that make the old man feel? He'd worked hard teaching Tanner the business and took pride in the fact his son would one day take over the dealership.

Tanner braced himself for the blasting.

"Way to go, son." Joe Peschke's big voice blasted over the speaker phone.

Huh? Tanner's eyes opened, and his hand fell to his side. Was this his father, praising him? Tanner frowned across the desk at the lead salesman.

Scott mouthed, *Told you so*.

"I knew you had it in you, son. You just needed the right angle. And boy, does that young lady have all the right angles."

"But, Dad—"

"For once your aptitude with the ladies has paid off." His father was on a roll now and couldn't be stopped. "That Janine is a gold mine. You were real lucky to find her."

"Yeah, Dad, I know. I was real lucky," he muttered.

Scott's lips twisted.

Tanner frowned. "Is there something in particular you wanted, Dad?" He hoped to end this conversation and get back to his day trading, so he could continue to build a comfortable nest egg to retire on when his father finally fired him from the used car business.

"Nope, just wanted to congratulate you on all the free publicity. By the way, Beans and I wanna know when you're airing the next episode of The Tarzan and Janine Show?"

Tanner muffled a groan.

"What was that you said, son?"

With a sigh, Tanner crossed his fingers. "Next Friday, Dad."

"Great, that's just great. I look forward to seein' you two. Funniest thing I'd ever seen. Beans thought it was an accident, but I told him it was your clever idea."

Not often did he receive praise from his

father, and Tanner...well...being Tanner, wasn't going to let him down over the phone. "Thanks, Dad. Well, I have to go."

"Hey Tanner, just one other thing," his father added.

What now?

"Leave all the sales to Scott and the other salesmen on the floor. You can concentrate on the marketing. If you can bring them in, the sales force can clinch the deals. Got it?"

"Got it," Tanner grinned. No more sales for him. "Gotta go, Dad. I'll talk to you later."

Pressing the speaker off button, Tanner sat staring at the phone for several minutes, stunned. His father had actually told him he was doing a good job. God, being appreciated felt good. Almost as good as his daydream, except for the one fly in the ointment.

Janine.

Tanner leapt to his feet, grabbed his car keys, and headed for the door.

"Where ya goin'?" Scott stepped aside to allow Tanner through.

"I've got just a few short days to cook up the next commercial, and I haven't got the key ingredient."

"And what's that?"

"Not what...who," Tanner said. "Janine Davis." No way was he telling his father he didn't have her contracted for the next commercial. He could handle this little challenge. How hard could convincing her to sign one little piece of paper be?

Chapter Five

Tanner stood outside Janine's apartment, clutching a bouquet of roses, a box of chocolates, and his flagging confidence. A lot was riding on this meeting, and he couldn't screw it up.

He jabbed a finger to the doorbell and then waited, his palms growing clammy. What if she said no? That single word could mean he'd be fired from the family business faster than he could say, "Hey Dad, a funny thing happened..."

After what seemed like an eon, the door finally opened and there she stood. Her hair curled in wild disarray around her face. Even with sad, red-rimmed eyes and smeared makeup in need of repair, she was still the most beautiful woman he'd ever seen.

Tanner sucked in a breath, his gut clenching liked he'd taken a hit in the solar plexus. His well-thought-out speech slipped from his thoughts like water through a sieve.

He stared at Janine, tongue tied and gripping the bouquet as though it was a lifeline in a sea of teenage, raging hormones. What was wrong with him? He wasn't asking her out or courting her. He wanted her to work for him. Yet an image of her climbing up his body and wrapping her legs around his waist shot through his mind, spurring his cock to immediate titanium hardness.

His gaze slipped downward from her face, taking in the fact that she wore a fuzzy old robe with pink rabbits and lambs scattered all over it. Her feet were encased in Bugs Bunny slippers, complete with six-inch ears, and she clutched a box of tissues.

"What do you want?" she asked in her breathy voice, then blew hard into the tissue in her hand.

"Are you all right?" Tanner asked in lieu of answering her question. As soon as he saw her, he'd forgotten what he'd come about. "You look like you're not feeling well."

"I'm fine." Her mouth tightened and her brow furrowed. Before she could say anything else, her bottom lip trembled and tears welled in her eyes. "I'm just freaking fine." Without warning, she slammed the door.

Tanner shoved his foot in the crack before the door closed all the way and winced. "Ouch." Had he been wearing anything else besides his cowboy boots, his foot would have been hurting a lot more.

"Serves you right." Janine scrubbed a hand over her wet cheeks. "I hope I broke it."

"Sorry, not today." Tanner pushed the door wide.

Janine shrugged and turned away, leaving

him to close the door behind himself.

Whatever had made her cry had something to do with him. Tanner tossed the flowers and chocolates on a table in the hallway and followed her into the living area. "What's wrong, Janine?"

"I'm too *flamboyant*." She snatched a tissue from a box on an end table and pressed it to her leaking eyes.

"In a beautiful way." Tanner removed the tissue from her fingers and dabbed at the tears coursing their way down her cheeks. "Is that a crime? I find it to be one of your more charming attributes."

"But you can't be too flamboyant and be a serious actress." She glanced up into his eyes, her own shadowed and as pathetic as a kicked puppy.

"And you want to be a serious actress." His chest squeezing tight, Tanner gave in to the urge to draw her into his arms.

Janine stiffened inside his embrace. "It's your fault."

"I'm sorry." He smoothed a hand over her hair, learning it was as soft as he'd imagined.

She sniffed, her hands on his chest, holding him back. Then she melted against him, resting her head against his chest, the tears flowing. "I wanted that part real bad."

"What part?"

She smacked a palm against Tanner's chest. "In Miller's play."

"If I could give it to you, I would." He tipped back her head and brushed the hair from her face. Then he pressed a gentle kiss to her forehead. Her skin was soft and her hair smelled of spring flowers. Tanner's gaze lowered to her mouth.

Her lips trembled.

That movement was Tanner's undoing. He gathered her closer in his arms and pressed his lips to hers.

Her mouth trembled beneath his then her head tilted, their noses aligned.

What started as a tender need to comfort her changed. And even though his better sense yammered in his ear about the fact he was pushing too fast, too hard, Janine's soft little moans built a full-fledged, raging inferno of desire.

Tanner decided not to think. *Just feel.* He slid his hands inside her fuzzy robe, his fingers meeting the bare skin around her midriff. The soft curve of her waist tempted him to discover more. He moaned into her mouth.

Janine's hands skimmed across his chest and around his neck, pulling him closer. Her lips parted and their tongues touched. But then she broke away, gasping for air.

They stared at each other for a long,

charged moment. Her big blue eyes were wide with shock. Her mouth formed a pretty pink O.

Tanner's body hardened, his breaths steadily deepening. With a slow deliberate move, one she could refuse if she had the mind, he shoved the robe over her shoulders. It fell silently to the floor, and Janine stood in front of him, naked and more beautiful than he'd imagined. "That Miller is a fool," he muttered, bending to trail a kiss down her jaw, following the long line of her neck to the sweet curve of her shoulder.

Her fingers threaded through his hair, and she moaned softly. "I wanted it so badly."

Fire ignited in every cell of Tanner's body as he stroked her back, his fingers sliding down to cup her rounded bottom. "I've wanted to do this since I met you." Then he lifted her, wrapping her long, slender legs around his waist.

Her head fell backward, hair falling over her back, brushing against his arms. "Don't get too attached. I plan on going to Hollywood." She gasped when he captured a perky nipple between his teeth. "Oh, man, that's *amaaaazzing*." She cupped the back of his head and pulled him closer.

He carried her across the floor and into her bedroom where he laid her on the mattress, her legs draping over the edge. For just a moment, his gaze took in the beautiful sight before him.

Rising to sit, Janine grasped the button at the waist of his jeans and struggled to free it, her fingers jerking at the fabric, ripping it loose. Then she slipped down the zipper, yanked to pull the material apart and down, and his cock sprang free.

Her eyes widened. "Oh, my."

"Anything the matter?" he asked, biting his cheek to hide his smile. Then he frowned. Was she disappointed?

"It's so big." She wrapped her hand around its girth and stroked him from tip to balls.

"Oh, baby, do that again and there'll be no stoppin'." He laid on the bed beside her, his fingers drifting along the curve of her waist.

"Did I ask you to stop?"

Her trademark scowl was so cute he felt his cock jerk. "No. But wait." He pulled out of her hands and pressed his forehead against hers. "We really should stop."

She sniffed. "On account of I'm such a horrible actress?"

He bit the tip of her nose. "On account I'm so darn hard, I won't last a minute inside you. And we really do need to talk."

Her eyes welled. "I don't want to hear anything you have to say."

Tanner fingered a loose strand of her hair then pushed it behind her ear. "You're mad at me?"

"I am."

"You've got a funny way of showin' it, ma'am." Because he didn't want her to stop crying or worse, start yelling, he pressed the solid ridge against her lower belly.

Her eyes widened and dried right up. "We really gonna do this?" she whispered.

"Only if you want it."

Her blonde brows lowered. "You always so accommodating to your co-stars?"

"Never had one before. But since it's you, I guess so."

White teeth bit into her full lower lip and Tanner nearly howled, but he kept it inside, waiting to see whether she showed even an inkling of hesitation. He didn't want her to regret being with him. He thought it just might kill him if she ever did.

Her lip slid from between her teeth, and she peeked from beneath the wet fringe of her eyelashes. "You owe me."

"Figurin' on takin' it out on my hide?" A man could only hope...

Janine trailed a finger slowly down the center of his chest.

Tanner leaned his torso to one side, letting her decide how far south that pretty painted finger scratched. When it scraped down the length of his rigid cock, he held his breath.

"Don't go making plans or anything. This doesn't mean a thing."

He'd hit her with the contract...after. "That a yes?"

She blinked once, and then gave an almost imperceptible nod.

Tanner breathed a sigh of relief then reached behind him, sliding his wallet free then dropping it in the center of her soft belly. "Behind the credit cards."

She picked up the wallet, flipping it open, and then dug for the condom, which she withdrew with two fingers. She held it up. "Were you a Boy Scout?"

He gave her a crooked grin and held up two fingers. "Want me to repeat the oath."

"No need." Her smile crept slowly across her face. "I was a Daisy. Doesn't mean I came prepared."

"I'm the one who came."

"Not yet, you haven't, cowboy."

The way she said the words, and that soft, sexy breathy voice nearly did him in. But he held himself still while she tore the packet with her pearly teeth then rolled the condom down his length.

When it was in place, she blinked and raised her gaze to his. "Put it inside me, Tanner. Do it quick."

Tanner rolled over her, waited as she parted her thighs and eased up her knees, then with a single prod found her entrance. He reached for both her hands and smoothed them up the bed, then laced his fingers through hers. "Hold on, sweetheart."

Janine gave him a small smile, and then gasped as he pushed inside.

Again, he rested his forehead atop hers as he tunneled inside. "Never felt this good. This hot."

"Bet you say this to all the girls."

"I don't. Really."

"I'll take your word."

He unlaced his fingers and pressed his palms on the bed, then pushed above her, watching her face as he stroked gently into her over and over.

Her thighs rose, hooked around his hips, and held tight. Her fingers dug into his back.

Tanner reached down and gave her a hard kiss. When he lifted his mouth, he said huskily, "You can make some noise."

"You need the encouragement?"

"All I need is you."

Her breaths were coming faster, but so were his. Her eyelids dipped lazily down. "Feels so good, Tanner Pesky. Feels damn good."

"Consider this the basic model. Then imagine it fully loaded."

A gust of laughter shook her. "Compare my ass to the chassis of a car, and I'll kick you to the floor."

He grinned. "No more car talk."

"Don't have the breath for it anyway."

Tanner reached beneath her and cupped her sweet curvy ass, bringing her closer as he stroked deeper and deeper. Her channel heated around him, moisture easing his way. With sweat beginning to slick his chest and back, he found his rhythm, closed his eyes, and tried not to think about how pretty she was or how perfectly they fit together.

This wasn't supposed to happen. They still needed to talk, but damn her fingers were scoring his shoulders, digging into his back, then his ass. He pumped faster, moving her and the bed, faster and faster.

When her breath hitched and her body bowed, tightening beneath him, he thrust harder until he felt the gentle convulsions rippling around his cock as she came. Only then did he let go, powering into her until he gave a husky shout. He rocked against her, the tension in his balls releasing in steady strokes.

When he opened his eyes again, she was staring upward. Her expression had him worried. "Did I hurt you?" He immediately withdrew and lay down beside her on the mattress, propped on one elbow.

"No. No." She looked everywhere but at

him. "This is not happening."

"I would have stopped, if you had said to." He smoothed a hand across her naked belly.

Janine shook her head, then turned her head and glared. "That's just it. I didn't. I can't believe I let it go this far. I have dreams! This isn't part of them." She sat up, pulling up the sheet to cover her naked body. "I'm going to Hollywood, damn it."

Back not quite to square one, Tanner lay propped on his side, a smile tugging at his lips. "Though I'd rather you stayed, I'm not stoppin' you."

"It's not you, it's me." She cast him an accusing glance. "I couldn't stop myself."

"And that's a bad thing?" He chuckled. "Felt pretty damn good to me."

"Exactly." She sighed and lay down beside him. "I should have gotten that part. I should be building my acting resume. Instead, I felt sorry for myself and fell into bed with you the first chance I got. It's all your fault." She rolled over and tapped a fist to his chest.

Tanner captured it and pressed his lips to her fingertips. "I don't know, I think you wanted it as badly as I did."

She frowned, her pretty brows winging inward. "I'm talking about Hal Miller."

Tanner grunted. "Who the hell is Hal Miller?"

"The director I auditioned for this morning."

"For the part you didn't get?"

"The director thought I was too flamboyant."

"How's that?" Tanner dragged his attention from her naked body, forcing his gaze around the room. Anywhere but at the naked woman, barely hidden beneath the sheet.

"Haven't you seen the newspapers?"

"Well actually, I have. That's one of the reasons why I'm here." Forgetting all his well-rehearsed speeches and promises not to sound too eager, he plunged in. "Janine, I need you."

Her eyes widened and her fists clenched. "That's your problem, buddy. I don't happen to need you. This is all a fantasy. I have plans and they don't include you."

Tanner shook his head and started over. "What I meant to say is that the dealership needs you."

"Oh." Her gaze dropped to his chest.

Had that been disappointment in her eyes? Tanner must have imagined it.

The next moment, Janine looked up, fire lighting her blue eyes. "So you came to ask me to come back to work for you?"

He didn't like the tone of her voice. A little too tight and mean. "Yes." He wanted to say so much more, but he was too afraid he'd louse things up even worse. And he wanted her to come back to work with him. Even more so after what had just happened.

"And what if I say no?"

His stomach churned. Failure wasn't an option. If Janine didn't come back to work for him, his father would fire him. On the other hand, if she did come back to work for him, he might lose more than his job. Somewhere between the mechanical bull and the sweet, hot sex he'd just enjoyed, his heart had veered onto a perilous path.

Tanner settled his hands on her shoulders and stared into her eyes, pouring every bit of his charm into his next words, fully aware of how much rode on her response. "Would you please come back to me, Janine?"

Heart be damned, he wanted this woman in his life. Not just for the dealership and his job, he wanted to spend more time in her company and this was the one way he could get it.

Janine hesitated, her gaze seeming to search his for something, then she shrugged. "I guess I'll have to, *since I don't have a part in Miller's play*. I need money to pay the rent."

"What about BS-squared?" As soon as the words left his mouth, Tanner could have kicked himself for reminding her of the other job offer.

Her chin lifted high. "Oh, I plan to take that one too. You're not getting an exclusive, you know. I'll do the next commercial, but I'm not guaranteeing anything after that. And this…" she waved a hand between their bodies, "won't happen again."

Tanner frowned. "How can you be so sure?"

"It won't happen," she said through tight lips. Her hand drifted halfway to his cheek before she jerked it back and tucked it beneath the sheet. She frowned mightily then captured his gaze with her own. "One more thing…"

"Anything." He held up his hand as if making a vow.

"I get a speaking part."

Tanner gave her a frown, thinking hard. He'd already seen how much she loved garbling up his last name. Not that it wasn't damn cute. He eased away the frown, eager to take whatever he could get from Janine. Somehow, he'd convince her to do more than the one additional commercial she'd promised. Tanner wanted her around a lot longer than one more show.

He'd just have to turn up the Tanner Peschke charm a notch. He shoved out his hand and grabbed hers. "It's a deal."

They shook, but Janine's brows drew together and her eyes narrowed in a thoughtful squint. "Oh, and Tanner...?"

"Yes, Janine?"

"No more monkeys."

* * *

Janine stood behind the bathroom door at Peschke Motors, breathing into a paper bag, attempting to avoid hyperventilating. Her crash-and-burn audition must have affected her more than she'd originally thought. She was completely petrified about speaking on live television after butchering her lines in front of Hal Miller.

Perhaps she should relent and let Tanner do all the talking. He was much more comfortable in front of the camera and managed to speak without shuffling words into incomprehensible gibberish.

Janine almost jumped out of her skin when a voice announced, "Five minutes, Miss Davis," from the other side of the door.

Another joined it. "Janine, it's me, Tanner. Can I come in?"

"No, go away," she answered.

"If you don't let me in, I'll go get the key and let myself in." A pause. "What's it going to be?"

Taking a deep breath with her face buried in the paper bag, Janine relented and opened the door, peering around the edge.

"What's wrong, Janine?" Tanner reached up to smooth her hair out of her face.

"Nothing," she said. A blatant lie. His look was so tender and concerned, she almost gave into her panic attack and launched herself into his arms. Almost, but a wave of fuzziness gripped her again and she leaned behind the door, breathing into the bag again.

"Are you afraid of the cameras today?"

"No," she managed.

"If it's the monkey, rest assured. Spunky's debut on commercials has made him so popular, I can't afford him any more. Did you know *America's Funniest Animals* want him to work with their announcer?"

"Freaking great," she grumbled. "I lose my clothes on television and the monkey's career is launched."

Tanner's mouth pursed. "Now do you want to practice your lines with me?"

"Lines?" Janine's eyes widened and she ducked behind the door again to breathe into the bag.

"Ahhhh. I see." Tanner said. "You're freaked because of your lines."

"I am not," she lied. "It's just that sometimes my words don't come out as planned."

"We can practice them if it makes you feel more comfortable." He pulled the script from his back pocket.

Janine took another deep inhale from the bag, then opened the door wider to look down at the script.

"I'll start off and introduce you," Tanner said, his deep voice a pleasant, soothing rumble. "Then when I say, 'don't take my word for it, ask Janine', that'll be your cue to begin with the lines you wrote. Want to try it?"

"Let's do it." Pushing aside her panic, Janine could felt a minuscule level of returning confidence. She was a professional. She shouldn't let a little rejection shake her. Meryl Streep didn't cower in a bathroom when she flubbed her lines.

Tanner launched into his part, reading it line for line. Janine silently read along until Tanner cued her in with, "...don't take my word for it, ask Janine."

Although she had the words memorized, she read them straight from the page, using the script as a crutch. "That's right, folks. Don't let the new car dealerships put the squeeze on you. Come to Pesky Motors—"

"Peschke," Tanner corrected.

"—where we'll take the pressure off. You'll breathe a sigh of relief at the no-pressure sales staff and quality cars to choose from." She glanced at Tanner, brows raised, waiting for him to jump in, but he was staring. "Tell them, Tarzan."

"Tanner," he murmured then glanced back down at the script. "That's right, come on by and let us show you the finest selection in pre-owned vehicles during our 'Squeeze Out Sale' tomorrow. Visit with Janine and the no-pressure sales staff at Peschke Motors—here's your next cue," he said. "Where we'll save you—" He nodded in her direction.

"Time and money. Join Tarzan and me, Janine, at Pesky Motors—"

"Tanner...Peschke."

"—for the 'Squeeze Out Sale' on Saturday. Only at Pesky Motors."

"Peschke." Tanner pressed his lips together as though trying to ward off a smile. "There, that wasn't so bad, was it?"

Returning his smile, Janine realized her head was clearer. "I guess I won't need this anymore." She wadded the paper bag into a ball and tossed it into a wastebasket. "Let's do a commercial." Shoulders squared, confidence returned in full force, she hesitated. "No monkeys, right?"

"No monkeys," Tanner confirmed.

Together, they turned to walk down the hall toward the showroom.

"I got a boa constrictor for this one," Tanner added.

Blood pounding in her ears, Janine stopped dead in her tracks. "A what did you say?"

"I got a boa constrictor for the commercial." He faced her, his brows furrowing. "Breathe, Janine."

She struggled to pull air into her constricted lungs. "A snake? As in huge and slimy?" A chill raced down her spine at the horror of touching a snake. "Is it alive?"

"Of course it's a snake. And yes it's alive. You'll be fine." He turned toward the showroom, moving swiftly down the hall. When he noticed she wasn't following, he looked around for her. "Are you coming?"

Janine wasn't going anywhere closer to the showroom. "Surely, you don't expect me to hold this snake?"

Tanner lifted a brow. " It's part of the gimmick."

"Gimmick, schmimmick." She planted both fists on her hips. "I'm not holding a snake. You got that Tanner Pesky?"

"Janine, you have to." He backtracked, tugging her fists from her hips so that he could hold her hands inside his. "I've already paid for the snake, and he really is a nice snake."

"I've always believed that the only good snake is a dead snake." She shook her head, the tips of her hair brushing her bare shoulders. "I won't do it."

Tanner's head drew back and he gave her a disapproving look. "Would a great actress like Marilyn Monroe or Joan Crawford refuse to show up on a set over a silly little snake?"

"I want Spunky back," Janine changed the subject. She flicked her hand toward the showroom. "Get Spunky."

Tanner held his breath, and his lips moved like he was counting. "I told you, we couldn't afford him anymore. Besides, you said you didn't want to do any more commercials with monkeys."

"I've changed my mind. A girl has a right to change her mind." Panic was setting in again. Her chest hurt with each breath. A snake? She'd never gotten close enough to a snake to touch one ever in her life. "No way!"

A cameraman appeared around the corner of the hallway. "Are you two ready? We have only two minutes until we're on."

Holy crap. Two minutes. Janine turned around and ran for the wastebasket. Grabbing the wrinkled paper bag, she opened the top and breathed into it. A snake? She breathed faster. *Think calm. You can do this. What would Marilyn do? The job, dammit.* Five more breaths into the bag and she straightened. "Okay, let's go."

"That's my girl." Tanner slipped an arm around her waist, firmly guiding her toward the showroom and the camera crew.

Janine heard him heave a huge sigh. Easy for him to be relieved, he didn't have to hold a damned snake.

Chills trickled down her spine. Well, one

thing was for certain. She wasn't worried about her lines anymore.

Chapter Six

With each step toward the lot, Tanner's confidence rose. They were poised to do another commercial, and Janine was still with him. The sales force had reported increased sales, and his father finally saw him as something more than a total screw up, without Tanner's having to tell him he'd scored big on the stock market. Life was certainly looking up.

I should do something special for Janine. She'd been game to come along for another even after their first two outings ended in disaster. The girl had spunk and a sense of humor, something most of the women he'd dated lacked.

Janine struggled to hold up under the heavy weight of the boa constrictor, and her face pinched, her hands shoving away the boa's mouth.

Tanner cringed and checked his watch, then relaxed. Janine would hold her ground, and he had no doubt she'd come through with a smile. Because that was Janine. He admired her desire to become an actress, and she played every part as seriously as if it were a starring role in a Broadway production.

Tanner wished he could find something

he liked doing as passionately as that. Day trading was something he was good at, but not something where he found passion. As for Peschke Motors, only since he'd taken over the marketing had he felt anywhere near fitting in with the family business. Frankly, he hated selling cars, but he loved working with people and finding ways to make them happy. Why did making a profit and satisfying people have to be mutually exclusive?

"Quiet on the set," the cameraman shouted. When everyone stopped talking, the man glanced at his watch and nodded at Tanner, then said, "Ready? Action!"

"Good evening, Austin. I'm Tanner Peschke, with Peschke Motors. Here at Peschke Motors, we pride ourselves in..."

Tanner's words flowed smoothly and things were going as planned. He held his breath when he got to Janine's cue. "...don't take my word for it, ask Janine."

The camera swung to take in Janine in her tight and sexy jungle outfit, struggling to retain the smile on her face. The tightness around her lips and the corners of her eyes were the only indication of her strain.

Tanner could tell her act was forced, but maybe the cameras wouldn't be as discerning.

"That's right, folks." Her voice shook, ever so slightly.

Tanner peered closer.

The poor woman was breathing awful fast, like maybe she could use that paper bag again.

"Don't let the new car dealerships put the *squeeze*—" Janine squeaked and twisted. The snake's head was dipping into the only crevice it could find, Janine's cleavage. Balancing the heavy snake on her shoulders, she tugged the head out of her bra, while smiling at the camera. Well, sort of smiling. Perhaps the gesture was more of a grimace, but she continued with her lines, barely missing a beat. "Come to Pesky Motors—"

"Peschke," Tanner corrected, automatically.

"—where we'll take the pressure off. You'll breathe a sigh of relief—"

Janine didn't look anywhere near breathing a sigh of relief. In fact, Tanner was worried she wasn't breathing *enough*.

"—at the no-pressure sales staff and quality cars to choose from." Her words tumbled out, increasing in speed until she practically spit out the lead-in for Tanner. "Won't you tell them, Tarzan?"

"Tanner," he corrected, turning back to the camera and plastering a smile on his face. Janine was pale, her skin tinged a bit on the green side. But this was live television. There wasn't much he could do at this point. They had a set number of minutes they had to fill.

The show must go on.

"That's right. Come on by and let us show you the finest selection in pre-owned vehicles during our 'Squeeze Out Sale' tomorrow. Visit me and Janine, and the no-pressure sales staff at Peschke Motors where we'll save you--"

This was Janine's cue and Tanner held his breath. And held his breath.

Nothing.

Turning toward Janine, he noticed what everyone else must have noticed at the same moment.

Someone shouted, "Do something, she can't breathe!"

The boa constrictor had wrapped itself around Janine's ribcage and neck, and her face had gone from pale to purple. Her eyes bugged out and she clawed at the huge snake squeezing the life out of her.

When Janine dropped to her knees, Tanner dove for her, catching her before she hit the ground.

She clutched his shirt, her eyes wide, frightened.

Tanner tore at the snake, to no avail. He had to do something. But what? How could he get the snake off? This wasn't in any Boy Scout book he'd ever read. Then he remembered the snake handler's words before he'd gone to get Janine for the commercial.

"If the boa gets too chummy, you know, tight, dangle the chicken in front of him. He loves chicken more than anything."

"Where's the chicken?" Tanner yelled. "Get the damned chicken."

Janine's eyes closed, her body going slack.

Praying they wouldn't be too late to revive Janine, Tanner counted the seconds. "Where's that damn chicken?" he screamed.

"Here it is." Scott raced to Tanner's side and shoved a birdcage containing one live chicken at Tanner.

"Don't give it to me, give it to the snake." Tanner's heart thundered ninety-to-nothing. He had to get the snake off of Janine, or there wasn't a chance in hell of reviving her.

"Huh?"

"Dangle the chicken in front of the snake's face." When Scott hesitated, Tanner just about lost it. "Do it, now."

Lifting the chicken, cage and all, Scott found the snake's head, pulled the chicken from the cage, and dangled it by the feet in front of the snake.

Tanner clawed at the beast while the chicken flapped and squawked, protesting its indignation at being held upside down. What was a matter of seconds felt like an eternity until the snake finally loosened its grip on

Janine and slithered toward the succulent fowl.

"Here snake, let the pretty lady go. This chicken is much more tasty." Scott backed away, an inch at a time

The boa slowly released Janine, one scale at a time.

As soon as the reptile cleared Janine's neck and ribcage, Tanner shook her. "Janine?"

No response.

All those years of CPR training in Boy Scouts finally came into use. Pressing his lips to Janine's, he breathed into her, filling her lungs with life-giving air, forcing them to expand. Tanner took another breath and breathed into her again, then checked for a pulse. It was faint, but there.

"Come on, Janine...breathe," he urged, taking another breath.

On the third round, Janine roused. Inhaling sharply, her body shook then went still again. Tanner waited for her to breathe on her own. When he didn't see her chest rise and fall, he leaned forward to breathe air into her again.

Janine wrapped her arms around Tanner's neck and what was supposed to be resuscitation transformed into a sock-bunching, toe-curling, incredibly passionate lip lock.

Tanner gathered Janine into his arms and deepened the kiss, feeling her body tense in response.

A round of applause rose around them, reminding Tanner they weren't alone. Apparently, the sound reminded Janine where they were, too.

"Are you alright?" Tanner pressed kisses to the side of her cheek, still holding her in his arms. "That snake didn't break anything, did it?"

Janine's body stiffened. Then her hands dropped from around his neck and inserted themselves between him and her, forcing him to lay her back on the ground.

Before he could react, he felt the sharp sting of her hand across his cheek.

"Tarzan, this Jane quits!"

* * *

"Been lookin' forward to this for an entire week, haven't you?" Beans twisted the top off a longneck bottle of beer and settled into the armchair next to Joe.

"You betcha." Joe rubbed his hands together, eager for the show to start. He punched the mute button on the television remote control to silence the voices of the night's popular sitcom. "Once again, Tanner didn't give me a clue as to what the commercial would be about. He did promise me that Janine woman would be in it again."

"That girl sure gives him a run for his money, if you ask me." Beans kicked up the footrest on the recliner and settled in. "Noticed the picture in the paper last weekend and the other Austin news channels were out in full force last Saturday. Wonder if he'll get the same response this time."

"Don't know. We'll just have wait and see." Joe checked his watch then the clock over the mantel of the fireplace. Both timepieces were exactly in sync. Placing an ear next to his wrist, he listened, satisfied at the ticking sound.

"No use wishin' your life away, Joe." Beans tipped his head in Joe's direction. "Relax, the boy'll do fine."

"I know that. I'm just anxious to see what new scheme he's concocted."

"How's the sales figures for the week?"

"Still too soon to tell. Have a lot of deals in the works, so it looks promisin'." Joe shot Beans a self-satisfied smile. "I'll sure enjoy that beer you're gonna buy me."

"The three months ain't up, yet. That boy of yours can still manage to lose the farm. I wouldn't be countin' your pull tabs—"

"Shhhh!" Joe pressed the mute button, then the volume, catching the tail of the announcement, "...brought to you by Peschke Motors."

Tanner stood in front of the cameras,

looking calm and happy. "Good evening, Austin. I'm Tanner Peschke, with Peschke Motors. Here at Peschke Motors we pride ourselves in..."

"Sure looks like his mother, doesn't he?" Beans remarked.

"Yup." Joe could see so much of Sarah in young Tanner. That girl had been the love of his life. At times, he missed her so bad it hurt. That's why, no matter how inept Tanner was at the car business, Joe couldn't turn him out. Tanner was just like his mother. They were both kind-hearted and attracted people by their warmth and sunny dispositions.

"What's that fool woman holdin'?" Beans interrupted Joe's reverie.

Peering closer, Joe's eyes widened. "Looks like a snake."

"What's that snake doin'?"

"I don't know, but that Janine is looking a little on the blue side."

Beans jumped from his chair. "Good God, she's goin' down."

Joe rose, his gaze glued to the television. "Geez, Tanner, do somethin'."He watched in morbid fascination as Tanner leaped into action, clawing at the snake wrapped around the girl squeezing her to death.

"Why's he yelling for a chicken?" Beans asked.

"I don't know, but Scott's got one."

Beans scratched his head. "Now what do you suppose they're gonna do? Hit the snake with it?"

"No, look, they're danglin' it like a carrot."

"I don't know about you, but I'd rather have the chick than the chicken."

"I only hope that snake prefers chicken," Joe said. When the snake let go of Janine and slithered toward the chicken, Joe let out the breath he'd been holding. "Holy cow, that was close."

Beans shook his head. "Hey, she's still lyin' there. Think she's dead?"

"Don't know, but Tanner's had enough CPR training, he oughta be able to help." Joe was glad to see all those years his wife had taken their son to Boy Scouts hadn't been a waste of time.

When Janine's arms wrapped around Tanner's neck, Beans chuckled. "Now, who's resuscitatin' who? Shouldn't they be comin' up for air soon? You'd think the girl would want some room to breathe."

"I don't think she wants to. In fact, I'd go so far as to say, she kinda likes my son." Joe straightened, his chest puffing out, straining the buttons on his shirt.

The kiss ended and the next thing Joe knew, Tanner was rubbing his cheek, a confused expression on his face.

Beans slapped his leg. "I'll be damned. If my eyes are seein' right, that girl just slapped your son."

"You're seein' right. What do you suppose it means?"

"A kiss and a slap, it could only mean one thing." Beans glanced his way.

Joe raised his hand to his cheek, his gaze sweeping back to another place, another time. "Sarah slapped me after I stole our first kiss." Joe whooped. "Those two kids are in love."

A smile spread across Joe's face and another graced Beans's. The two men executed a loud high-five and adjourned to the kitchen for a cold beer to celebrate.

Chapter Seven

The phone hadn't stopped ringing since Janine returned to her apartment, and her answering machine had maxed out at twenty messages.

Tanner had insisted on a quick trip to the emergency room where the doctor pronounced her fit as a fiddle and congratulated her on her performance on The Tarzan and Janine Show.

What was wrong with the people of Austin? Couldn't they see the commercials for what they were? Each airing had been an unqualified disaster.

Janine managed to put off dealing with the messages while she showered and put on a soft pink babydoll nightie and her favorite bunny slippers. Fortified in comfortable clothing, she stepped out into the living room, squaring her shoulders for the onslaught of messages she'd have to wade through.

As quickly as possible, she blew through them, some from friends, wishing her well on her career as a commercial actress. Some of the calls were from men she'd met or dated in the past, asking her out. The last message was from her mother.

"Janine, it's your mother. Honey, are you

all right? Call me."

Janine erased all the messages, put away the few groceries she'd grabbed on the way home, and then settled in a chair, before she picked up her home phone and dialed her mother.

"Janine, honey. Thank God, you're okay."

"Hi, Mom."

"Tell me that was all for show. That snake didn't nearly kill my baby, did it?"

Janine didn't like to worry her mother. The woman had worked hard all her life, worrying about where the next meal came from, and if her cancer would return. Janine didn't have the heart to reveal that her only daughter had almost bit the big one on set. "No, Mom, it wasn't for real. I'm fine."

"That Tanner Peschke is a good looking man, don't you think? Is he married?"

"Mom, I'm not looking for a husband. I'm not giving up my dreams for any man."

"Baby, I don't want you to give up your dreams." Her mother sighed. "I also don't want you to give up on love. It can be a very beautiful thing between a man and a woman."

"Yeah, but love doesn't always pay the rent." Janine regretted her outburst as soon as it left her lips. "Look, Mom, we've been over this before. You gave up your dreams to marry my father. I'm not giving up mine."

"I didn't give up my dreams, sweetheart. I chose a different dream."

Janine sighed. She'd heard it all before—and still didn't believe her mother's words. "Okay. Is there anything else you wanted to talk about?"

"I'm just worried about you, baby. This is the second job you've started in the past two weeks. Is there anything going on you need to talk about?"

Besides being fired from one job after being tossed off a bucking bull and hired into the circus of commercials with one hot used car salesman cowboy...no. "I'm good, Mom. At the rate I'm saving, I should have enough to get out to L.A. soon."

"Oh." Her mother sighed, her voice going quiet. "I know that you need to do what you need to do, but it will be lonely without you here in Austin."

"I don't even know when it'll be, but you can bet I'll send for you as soon as I land a paying position."

"I love you, sweetheart."

"I love you, too. Gotta go. I have an audition in the morning I want to get there early."

"Break a leg, honey," her mother said. "And remember, I wouldn't change a thing about my life and my choices."

As soon as she clicked the off button, her

phone rang, and Tanner Peschke's name appeared in the caller ID display.

Her pulse quickening, Janine hesitated. Her conversation with her mother was still fresh in her mind.

Five rings later, her thumb remained hovering over the talk button, and she still hadn't answered. Finally, she set the phone in its cradle and strode for her bedroom. If he wanted to get in touch with her, he could leave a message.

The ringing ceased and the answering machine picked up.

"Janine, answer your phone. I know you're at home."

Tanner's voice over the telephone had the same effect it had in person.

Her footsteps faltered, her body flushed with heat, and her heart banged against her ribs. Damn the man. Why couldn't she ignore him like all the other men who'd come and gone in her life?

"Janine." The way he said her name sounded like creamy chocolate dripping over her skin.

Keep walking, girl. She took another step. Instead of taking her to her bedroom and a cool shower, she backtracked to the kitchen. A cup of hot tea would help.

As she passed the phone it beeped, indicating the end of the message on the answering machine.

Janine let out the breath she'd been holding and entered her kitchen, yanking a mug from the cabinet, and filling it with water.

Halfway to the microwave, the phone rang again, and Janine nearly dropped the cup.

Five more rings and the answering machine picked up.

"Janine, I just want to talk to you. I need to know you're okay. Answer your phone. Please."

Ignore it. Forget how he makes you feel when his hands skim across your naked skin. You don't need a man. He'd just slow you down in the pursuit of your dreams. As though her hand had a mind of its own, it reached out and snatched the phone from the cradle.

The answering machine beeped the end.

"Janine? Are you there?"

For a moment, her voice lodged in her throat. She swallowed hard, her body awash with need. "I told you I quit."

"Will you go out with me for a drink? We can go somewhere neutral."

"No."

"I promise not to touch you unless you want me to."

Oh, dear God, she wanted him to touch her. That was the problem. "I can't. I'm too tired."

"Then let me come by. I'll only stay a minute. I'm worried about you, after the snake and all."

"I'm fine."

"Prove it to me. Let me come visit."

"No. I'm about to go to bed." Wrong thing to say. The images the word *bed* ignited in her imagination, and her breathing grew more ragged.

A knock on the door made Janine jump. "I can't talk anymore. Someone's at my door."

She should have pressed the end button right then, instead she walked toward the door, hoping Tanner would end the call.

"Don't hang up on me, Janine."

Another knock at the door.

"I have to." Janine stopped and leaned her forehead against the cool wood of the front door. She swallowed hard against a dry throat. "I'm not coming back to work for you. Look, Tanner, I need to answer the door. I don't want to see you anymore. I'm done."

"Please, Janine. Open your door." The voice came through the receiver pressed to her ear, an echo coming from the other side of the door.

Janine pressed her free hand against the wood, moisture pooling between her thighs. Holy hell, he was on the other side of the door, and she wanted to open it so badly, her hands shook.

"Please, open the door," Tanner whispered in her ear.

She reached for the handle, turning it slowly, realizing what the action meant and helpless to stop herself.

The door swung open as if in slow motion.

On the other side, Tanner leaned in the doorframe, a sexy smile sliding up his cheeks.

"Oh, you!" Janine pushed the door closed in his face. "You *knew* I'd open the door."

"No, Janine, really. " The smile wiped clean, Tanner stuck his foot in the door to keep her from locking him out. The door bounced hard against Tanner's foot. "Holy Jesus, Mother of God."

She clapped a hand over her mouth. "Tanner? Oh, sweetie, I'm sorry. I didn't mean to hurt you." Janine dropped to her haunches beside him, her brows V'd. "Are you okay? Did I break it?"

Tanner rubbed the injured foot. "I'll live." He reached out to grab her hand. "And for the record, I didn't think you'd open the door."

She stared hard into his face and damned if she didn't believe him. "Then why were you smiling like the cat that ate the can of berries?"

"Canaries," he corrected. "And I was

smiling because I got to see you again. Outside of work. And you're even more lovely now than in your Jane outfit."

She glance down at her breasts, clearly visible through the sheer pink fabric. The nipples puckered under Tanner's scrutiny. Janine crossed her arms and frowned. "Some gentleman. You should have called before you came."

Eyebrow quirked, he grinned. "Technically, I did."

* * *

"I can't believe I let him talk me back into this cheesy outfit, especially after that snake tried to kill me." Janine paced in the bathroom at Peschke Motors Saturday morning, berating herself for her Tanner weakness.

That was all she could figure. Every time he came near her, she totally lost all focus and sense of reason. If he had a mind to, he could talk her into walking off a cliff. As crazy stupid as she had been lately, she'd probably do it. What was it about him that made her absolutely addlepated?

A tap on the door was followed by a familiar voice. "Janine?"

She fumbled with the canister of hairspray she'd been holding. As if thinking about Tanner conjured him. Geez, she needed to put some distance between them. She had to tell him she couldn't do any more commercials. If she kept doing them, she might never land a real acting role in the theatre or movies.

This was it. She was going to tell him. She sucked in a deep breath and opened the door. "Tanner, I need to talk to you."

"These are for you." Tanner handed her a gorgeous bouquet of brilliant red roses. "What is it you wanted to talk about?"

With velvety soft blooms in her face and their heavenly scent wafting beneath her nose, Janine did what most red-blooded American woman would do in just such a situation. "I don't remember."

"Did I tell you how glad I am you decided to come today?" His warm gaze met hers.

"No, you didn't."

"Well, I am, and you look fantastic." His glance skimmed the length of her body.

Heat sang through her blood, reminding her of just how Tanner had persuaded her to perform in the next commercial. Her lungs squeezed as tightly as if the boa constrictor was still wrapped around her middle. Not again would she fall victim to the Peschke charm. She absolutely refused to settle for less than her dream.

Pushing her lusty thoughts to the back of her mind, she clutched the bouquet to her chest like a shield, glad it kept her fingers otherwise occupied. *Keep it impersonal. Don't touch the sexy cowboy.* "You've seen me in this outfit before."

"I know, but you look better every time."

Call it woman's intuition, déjà vu, whatever, she knew he was up to something. "What do you want, Tanner?"

Tanner stepped closer, removing the bouquet from her grip, setting it on a table in the hallway. With her hands free, she could have blocked his advance, but they moved of their own accord. When Tanner's arms wrapped around her waist, her own wound around his neck.

What was wrong with this picture? Janine couldn't recall exactly what she was supposed to tell Tanner. Somehow she knew it wasn't how wonderful his lips felt against hers or how his hands roaming across her bare back would feel even better in more...intimate places. "What are you doing to me?"

"It's got to be that outfit," he said. "Does it make you feel as sexy as you look?"

It isn't the outfit, it's you. Janine's eyes widened. Did she say those words or were her thoughts that loud?

"I do have something to tell you." He nuzzled her neck.

"No snakes," she breathed, her knees going weak.

"No snakes," he agreed. "I have a question." He bent close, his lips an inch away from hers.

"Yes," she breathed.

"Yes?" Easing back his head, Tanner grinned. "I haven't asked the question, yet."

Janine had to physically shake herself out of her Tanner-stupor. The only way to do that was to put space between them. She forced her arms to drop from around his neck and stepped away from the spellbinding man. There. That ought to do it. But her errant body still swayed in his direction. The traitor. "What's the question?"

"A local talk show host called and asked if we'd like to be on her show this morning?"

Janine's heart leaped into her throat. "What did you say?"

"I said a local talk show——"

"I heard what you said." She grabbed the front of his shirt. "I asked the wrong question. I meant what did you say to him?"

"Her. Apparently we've gotten so much coverage on the news, we're becomin' local celebrities." Tanner grinned. "Can you believe it? She wants to bring us on her show and ask us questions. You know, an interview about our life histories."

"That won't fill a show. Mine is incredibly boring." She circled a hand in the air. "I haven't even made it past the Austin city limits, yet."

"Mine too, but I'm sure she'll manage. And what will it hurt? It's free advertisin' for the dealership."

"It may be advertising for the dealership, but what does it buy me?"

"You're gettin' your face out there. People walkin' down the streets of Austin will know you by name."

Janine snorted. "Yeah, like they already do? Since last weekend, I've been called Jane more times than I can remember."

"Think of it as gettin' the chance to set the record straight." When she didn't respond, he went on. "You could tell the world—well, the greater Austin area in this case—about your desire to be a serious actress."

What would it hurt? It would get her name straightened out and give her more airtime. Maybe she wasn't destined to be discovered in the theatre. Perhaps she could be discovered while doing commercials. They'd see how photogenic she was and offer her parts of greater distinction, something worthy of an Academy Award. A thrill of excitement winged through her veins.

Tanner cleared his throat. "Well?"

Janine came back to earth from the stage at the Academy Awards celebration in her mind. "I suppose it would be all right."

Before she could protest, Tanner grabbed

her shoulders, planted a kiss on her lips, and strode away.

Tanner Pesky was like one of those cartoon characters. *Which one was it? Oh yes, the Tasmanian Devil.* Whirl in, sweep a girl off her feet, and whirl out again. Janine had to take a few deep breaths to regain her balance before she could walk out through the showroom and into the car lot.

The talk show sounded interesting. She wondered what questions would be asked, wishing she could prepare her answers ahead of time. Oh well, whatever happened, happened. She just hoped the interview wouldn't be any more career-limiting than chasing monkeys or getting choked by a snake.

* * *

"Welcome to Austin Live, I'm Lisa Grant. Today I'm pleased to introduce Tanner Peschke and Janine Davis, Austin's own Tarzan and Jane."

Tanner cringed behind his pasted-on smile. That wasn't going to make Janine happy. She'd hoped to make this appearance count toward setting the record straight on her name and acting career. He didn't mind being called Tarzan because the moniker was good for the business, but he knew how Janine felt about being called Jane.

When he stole a glance at her face, he

was surprised to see her smiling, albeit a strained smile, but a smile nonetheless. Pride and admiration swelled in his chest. She was a born actress, not one to be swayed by insensitive hosts or car salesmen. Janine knew what she wanted and, dammit, she wasn't going to stop until she got it.

Tanner shook his head and smiled wryly. He wished it could be so easy. If only he knew what he wanted to do. All his life he'd been raised with the understanding he would take over the car business from his father. But, the closer the reality came, the more he pushed it away. He'd made his first million shortly after graduating from college. With the help and encouragement from the Texas Billionaire's Club, he'd stockpiled millions in stocks and real estate. But that was all play money. He still didn't know what he wanted to do—what would make a difference. Selling used cars in the family business just wasn't it. His promise to his mother kept him holding on.

No longer a kid to be told what to do, Tanner knew he could make his own decisions. The primary problem was he didn't know what occupation would hold his interest. Day trading he could do anytime, anywhere. To him, the activity wasn't a real job and having your destiny preordained by family obligation tended to limit your perception of options.

"Tanner, do you have a professional writer and choreographer stage all your commercials?" Lisa's question shook Tanner from his internal reverie.

"No, Lisa, I write all the copy." Tanner glanced at Janine's frown and added, "with my partner, Janine."

Lisa smiled briefly in Janine's direction but returned her attention to Tanner. "That's amazing. So you planned everything that has happened thus far on your commercials?"

"Not exactly," Tanner hedged.

"You mean the monkey stealing Jane's top was an accident?"

"Absolutely," Janine answered quickly. "And the name's Janine."

"And the boa putting the squeeze on you wasn't just to sensationalize the commercial?" Lisa continued with the microphone wavering between the two.

Tanner caught Janine's gaze and recalled the fear lumped in his throat when he'd thought he couldn't save her from that blasted snake. "No, that was not supposed to happen."

"Surely, the kiss was planned," Lisa stated.

His gaze held Janine's. "No, it just..."

"...happened." Janine's breathy voice finished his sentence as naturally as if she could hear his thoughts.

Lisa looked from Tanner and back to Janine. "Helloooo." The hostess waved her hand between them to get their attention. "Whose idea was it for the theme of the commercials and the costumes?"

"Mine." With great effort, Tanner turned his attention to the host.

"The media has nicknamed you both Tarzan and Jane." Lisa tipped her head, her gaze on Tanner. "You have Janine wearing a Jane outfit. Why aren't you wearing a Tarzan loin cloth?"

Startled by the question, Tanner was at a loss for words.

"Because he's a sexist chicken," Janine answered, her eyebrows quirking upward.

What was she up to?

"Isn't that a little degrading to be the only one in such a skimpy costume while doing the commercials?" Lisa's attention moved to Janine.

"As a matter of fact, I've been meaning to talk to you about that." Janine's voice held a dangerous tone.

Tanner would have considered the tone sexy had it not been directed at him along with a narrow-eyed stare. He gave both women a winning smile. "Now, wait a minute, ladies. It's not fair. There's two of you against the one of me. This isn't some battle of the sexes. Besides, the costume makes the commercial." Tanner's smile turned cajoling at Janine's fierce glare. "Look, honey, you can't *not* wear it. That would take away from the theme and ruin the feel."

"Honey?" Her voice rose and she crossed her arms over her luscious breasts. "I'm not wearing it anymore."

Tanner gulped. The image her statement generated certainly was not what she had intended. He envisioned her in nothing at all. His more attentive parts perked up. As casually as possible, he crossed his legs to hide the evidence. "Janine, be reasonable." Tanner pasted on *his* most reasonable smile. He could kick himself now for suggesting they do the talk show. If Janine refused to wear the Jane outfit, who would watch the commercials?

Janine sniffed, and then gave him a look that made him worried.

"Look, honey, I'll make a deal with you," she said in her breathy voice, leaning close.

His gaze fixed on her lush mouth. "Something tells me I'm not gonna like it."

The corners of her lips curved and her blue eyes glinted. "I'll continue to wear the Jane outfit, if you wear a Tarzan loin cloth."

His mouth opened, ready to tell her just how ridiculous the idea was.

"That's perfect." Lisa whooped and clapped her hands." I could just see it now. Tarzan and Jane take Austin by storm."

Tanner glared at Lisa. "No way."

Janine's eyebrows rose. "What's the matter, Tanner...you chicken?"

"No, but what self-respecting man would be caught dead in a loin cloth in public?"

"And it's alright for a woman to be seen in the outfit you have me wearing? Tsk, tsk, Tanner." Her blonde hair swayed as she shook her head. "Haven't you heard of equality?"

Outnumbered and outmaneuvered, Tanner knew he wouldn't win this argument. Come Friday, he'd be wearing a damned loin cloth.

* * *

"Here's one," Janine called over the racks of costumes crisscrossing the floor of the costume shop.

An answering mumble alerted her to Tanner's location. She found him hiding behind the Henry VIII costumes, a frown permanently etched between his brows. "Oh come on, quit crying. A deal's a deal."

"Look, I'll let you choose the next animal for the commercial if you forget all about this cockamamie idea," he said, his gaze pleading with her.

Janine shook her head and crooked her finger, indicating he should follow her to the changing room.

But, he stood fast.

She dangled the scrap of fabric pinned to the clothes hanger. It was the size of a handkerchief. A folded one, at that.

"No way, you can't really expect me to wear that?" he said, horror jamming his eyebrows halfway up his forehead.

"Why not? It's as presentable as the Jane ensemble."

Tanner lowered his voice and bent toward her. "Not to be bragging or anything, but it's not big enough."

Well, Tanner had that right. The man was well equipped as he'd proved the night before in her apartment. Still, she wanted to see him in the loin cloth. Her pulse pounded in anticipation "Prove it." She held out the scrap of fabric. "Come on. Don't be a baby."

"I certainly don't need to prove anything to you."

"Well, then stop your belly-aching and get in there."

When he still didn't budge, she gave him a stern look. "You're not going to go back on your promise, are you? You gave your word in front of God and everybody on public television. If you don't show up in a loincloth, the entire city of Austin will know you can't keep your promises. Then who would buy cars from you or your business?"

Tanner sagged, his willpower crumbling.

She could see by the disgruntled look on

his face.

"I'm swearin' off all women," he muttered. "They're nothing but trouble."

She held back a grin. "Come on Romeo, try this on."

Tanner looked like a little boy being forced to stand in a corner for some infraction.

"It won't bite, you know." She dangled the loincloth.

"That's where you're wrong. It does bite. It bites big time."

Janine found a chair and pulled it over in front of the dressing room. This was a show she didn't want to miss. Her mouth was already watering. Tanner was a handsome man with a body any girl would enjoy watching.

Tanner ducked into the changing room, a scowl making him look fierce and even cuter.

"So Tanner, how long have you been doing commercials for the dealership?" Talking to a door was somewhat easier than talking to his face. She didn't get quite as distracted.

"For the last year or so." His voice was muffled by the door and possibly a shirt going over his head.

"Have you thought of doing them for a living?"

A loud thump rattled the wall and shook

the door. Tanner let loose a muttered curse. "Not really. Why should I?"

"Well for one, you're pretty good at being in front of the camera."

"Naw, it's just for fun. When you grow up in a family-owned business, you have to find your fun somewhere. This is mine. What about you? What made you want to be an actress?"

"I guess I spent so many years watching all the oldies on the television and the actresses seemed larger than life. I always wanted to be as good as a Carol Lombard or Joan Crawford."

"Or Marilyn Monroe?"

Janine sighed. "Yes. They were great, weren't they?"

"Don't you ever want to settle down and raise a family?"

"No." She couldn't afford to let emotions get in the way of attaining her career goals.

"Excuse me for asking," came the voice from the other side of the door. "Damn. Which end is up on this thing? What did you do, find the smallest one in the store?"

"No, actually it was the biggest." She smiled at his obvious discomfort with the whole dress-up thing.

"Why are you so set against raising a family? I thought every woman's dream was to have children and a house with a picket fence."

Janine shook her head, even though he couldn't see her through the door. "You've been watching too many old movies too."

"So you want a career and no family?"

"I didn't say that, you did," she said.

"Then humor me, what is it you want?"

What was it she wanted? "For as long as I can remember, I've wanted to be an actress, and I plan to be successful at it if it kills me. I won't sacrifice my dreams for a family."

"Sounds like some history behind that comment."

For a few moments, Janine didn't reply. Somehow talking to a door was easier than to Tanner in person. "My mother was nineteen when she got married. All her life, she'd wanted to be a commercial pilot, but when she got married, she gave up her dreams. And what did that choice get her? A divorce and one little girl to raise on her own, making barely more than minimum wage."

"Was it her choice to leave him or his?"

"What does it matter? She lost her dreams when she married." Her hands tightened in her lap. "I will attain my dreams before I decide on anything else. Otherwise, I'll regret it for the rest of my life."

"Did your mother regret it?"

Funny, but Janine had never asked her. "I

don't know," she answered in all honesty. "She says she doesn't, but what are you gonna tell your kid? Sweetie, I gave up everything for you, but now I take it back? "

"Perhaps you should talk to her about it. Ask her if she really doesn't regret it."

"I will, next time we talk." Had her mother regretted her life? She'd worked very hard to take care of her little girl.

Janine remembered when her mother had been battling breast cancer. She'd been so sick with the chemo treatments and thought she was dying. Lillian Davis had gripped her daughter's hands and stared up from the pillow. "Promise me," she said, her voice barely above a whisper, but intense enough to resonate like a scream.

"Yes, Mamma, anything," Janine had said, her eyes filled with tears.

"Promise me you'll follow your dreams," she'd said. "I want you happy."

"But how will I know if they are the right ones?"

"Listen to your heart," she'd said. Her grip loosened and her hand fell to the sheets. "Promise."

"I promise Mamma. I love you," Janine had said.

"I love you, too, Janine. I always have," she said.

Those were the words her mother had

spoken at the lowest point of her life. Yes, she'd recovered and had been in remission for nearly five years. In that time, Janine had lived up to that promise, clinging tightly to her dreams, determined to make them happen. The goal she intended to reach was for herself as well as her mother, and nothing would get in the way.

"Why they make these dressing rooms so small is beyond me. I feel like I'm Houdini trying to wiggle out of a straightjacket in a submerged coffin," Tanner groused.

Shaking free of the depressing mental images of her mother, sick and weak, Janine could visualize what was going on in the little closet of a dressing room. The sound of a zipper immediately set her heart racing. The only thing between her and a naked Tanner was a door. If she were the bold and brazen type, she might just open that door and let herself in.

A noise behind her brought her back to earth. She realized she was halfway out of her seat, acting on the images racing through her mind.

Glancing around, Janine spied two little old ladies browsing through the biker costumes.

"I don't know, Louise. Do you think it's a bit too... racy?"

"Not at all. It'll spice up the retirement

village costume party, if you ask me," Louise said.

"Still, I don't want to be responsible for one of the older gentlemen having a heart attack."

"Oh, Beatrice, they could use a little excitement to juice up their pacemakers."

Janine smothered a giggle at the interplay between the older women.

"What do I have to pay you to get me out of this deal?" Tanner asked through the door.

"There's not enough money in the world."

"This thing is entirely too small."

Janine smiled, resisting the urge to laugh out loud at the pathetic sound of his voice. "And mine is much bigger? Come on, quit being such a baby. Let me see."

"All right, but I'm tellin' you, I'm not wearin' this in public. Is the coast clear?"

Janine looked around. The two old ladies had worked their way toward the dressing room. By the looks on their faces, they'd heard Tanner's last comment. Their gazes were zoomed in on the dressing room door as if it were a prize door in a game show.

Crossing her arms and leaning back in her chair, Janine thought of the monkey, the bra, and the killer snake. "Coast is clear," she sang with a smile.

Chapter Eight

"Well, boy, how's it going?" Joe Peschke strode into Tanner's office like he owned the place. *Because he does.* Tanner was not in the mood to hear his father tell him how much of a failure he was. His dignity was still recovering from the bruising it had taken in the costume shop.

When he'd stepped out of the dressing room in not much more than his birthday suit, he'd expected to model for Janine... only Janine. He'd seen what he thought was a glint of appreciation light her eyes. After hearing the gasps of surprise from the other two women in the audience, he now realized it was a glint of amusement he'd mistaken for appreciation.

Janine had gulped before saying, in a shaky voice, "My, my, I'd say it's a perfect fit, wouldn't you, ladies?"

Any starch in his libido had been thoroughly erased by the seventy-year-old women's wolf calls. Instead of saying something completely suave and nonchalant, his hands formed a fig leaf over his privates, and he ducked back into the dressing room, slamming the door behind him. So much for manly dignity.

"Come on out here, stud muffin," one of the blue-hairs yelled. "We won't bite."

"We might pinch a little, but with our arthritis, it won't hurt much," said the other.

"I'm not comin' out until they're gone." He'd hopped up and down, cramming legs into his jeans, costume and all. No telling what those women were capable of. They'd stared as if he was some juicy side of beef. Who knows, they might have tried to open the door and take a sample taste.

Fully dressed, with his socks stuffed, one in each pocket, and his jeans hanging out of his quickly donned boots, Tanner marched out of the dressing room.

"There's no way I'm gonna get in front of a camera in this thing." He passed Janine, heading for the sales counter.

"Why?"

"It's not decent." He slapped a hundred dollar bill on the counter, giving the cashier a cool stare. "I'm wearin' the costume out. Keep the change."

"It looked like a perfect fit to us, right, ladies?" Janine turned to the older women. Whistled wolf calls from the ladies standing by the door were her answer. "See? You look great."

"I don't have a tan in all the right places," he argued.

"We can get some of that instant tanning

lotion."

Damn Janine for finding a solution to every obstacle.

"I'll smear it on," volunteered one of the old ladies.

"I won't do it," he insisted.

Janine had stood at the end of the counter with a fist on one hip. "Wimp."

"Have you heard a word I've said in the last ten minutes?" Tanner's father's voice brought his reverie to a screeching halt.

With a hard shake of his head, Tanner tried to concentrate on the man standing by the window. For the first time in years, Tanner looked at him as something other than the dominating patriarch of the family and business. Why was he so intimidated by the man? Janine's taunt echoed in his mind. Wimp? Was that the problem? Was he afraid of the man?

His eyes narrowing, Tanner took a closer look, noticing the wrinkles around his father's eyes. His thick hair was more salt than pepper, and he moved with a little stiffness in his right leg. Damn, his father was starting to look old. Tanner thought back to his father's last birthday. All the sales staff had decorated his office with black balloons and buzzards because it was his sixtieth. Somehow, the fact had escaped Tanner's attention that his father was getting older. The man was a rock, incapable of weakness. How could he allow himself to get older? Hell, he was only a few years away from retirement age.

"I must say I'm impressed with the progress you're makin'." Joe Peschke stood with his back to Tanner as he gazed out on the lot filled with customers and salesmen. "With Scott runnin' the sales and you runnin' the marketing, you have a chance at meeting the three-month challenge I set out for you."

Tanner blew out a deep breath. "That's what I'm aiming for, Dad."

His father turned to face him, the corners of his mouth turning up in a sad smile. "Your mother would be proud."

A tug in the region of his heart quieted Tanner's ever-glib tongue. He didn't know how to respond to his father's comment, so he just smiled and shrugged. He noticed his father hadn't said he was proud of him. But the statement was pretty darned close to the praise he'd always craved.

Joe's eyes narrowed. "In fact, you're a lot like her."

Tanner smiled softly at the image that lingered in his memories of his mother. "Everyone's always said I take after Mom."

"Yes, you do." Joe's eyes glazed over.

Tanner knew that look. The same look his father got each time he reminisced about his departed wife. Then his eyes cleared and he focused on Tanner.

"But more than that, you have her flighty nature. She loved everyone and everyone loved her. On her, it worked. On you..." Joe shook his head sadly. "On you, the trait's not necessarily a good thing. In car sales, you'll be taken advantage of in a heartbeat. It's a tough business and you have to be on your toes at all times. Think you can handle that, son?"

"Yes, sir," Tanner answered automatically, his father's lecture about the business being tough—an old lecture he'd been subjected to since before puberty.

Joe cleared his throat, effectively ending his sermon. "So, what's next? Lions jumpin' through flaming hoops, trained dancin' bears? Beans and I have a bet going. I say lions, he says alligators."

Tanner glanced out the window and smiled. A huge truck was backing into the lot as they spoke. "It's a surprise, Dad. A big surprise," he added.

Joe's gaze followed Tanner's. "What are they deliverin' now? All large deliveries are usually made on Mondays and Tuesdays. Do I need to have a talk with Rudy in shippin'?" Joe was halfway to the door, opening his mouth to shout orders when Tanner stopped him.

"I placed this order, Dad," he said.
"For a Friday?"

"Yes, Dad." Taking his father's elbow, he led him toward the side door where he usually parked. He didn't want him on the lot when they filmed the next commercial. Nor did he want him to see the latest prop until he was safely home and relaxed. "Trust me, Dad. I know what I'm doin'."

"If you'd known what you were doin', I'd have turned over the business to you already," he blustered.

Tanner's lips tightened. "Thanks, Dad." So much for his father being proud of him. The man still didn't have faith in him as a businessman. Oh well, Rome wasn't conquered in a day. Tanner had two months to topple his father's opinion of him, and, if things stayed on track, he'd show him what he was made of. Then maybe his father would say those yearned-for words about pride.

Joe Peschke was driving out of the lot when a two-door hatchback painted in garish tiger stripes passed him on the way in. The little car wove through the maze of parked cars and screeched to a halt at Tanner's feet.

A slightly hefty woman in the fortyish age-range stepped out of the car. "Tanner, *bonsoir*," she said in a fake French accent, wiggling her fingers in greeting. She reached into the back of the car and lifted out a suitcase the size of Rhode Island. "Are you ready to get tanned all over?" She carried the suitcase as if it weighed less than a briefcase.

Tanner cringed. "Hi, Bridgett. No, I'm not ready," he grumbled.

The camera crew for the commercial was already setting up in the lot. This time, Tanner really hoped the city of Austin wouldn't actually be watching. Especially since he was to make his debut in a loincloth. How Janine talked him into this, he didn't know, but he wasn't feeling altogether good about being seen in his altogether. A man had to be absolutely secure about his manhood to parade around like Tarzan, either that or he had to have a balls of steel.

Tanner led Bridgett to his office, pulling closed the window. "You can set up in here. How long will it take?"

"Ten minutes, tops." She grinned, and with the flick of a latch, she opened the case and pieced together what looked like a gurney. A shaky one at that.

Tanner had never experienced butterflies in his stomach, but he had an entire flock of them churning away at what he suspected would be an ulcer by the end of this shoot.

With the enthusiasm of a man marching toward the guillotine, he entered the men's room and slipped out of his clothes and into the skimpy loincloth.

Tanner raked a hand through his dark hair, and shrugged, then he threw a t-shirt over his head. After pulling his jeans on over the offensive outfit, he padded barefooted down the hall to his office.

The room was shrouded in smoky darkness, burning incense and candles making it more like a bedroom than an office. No, not a bedroom, more like an altar in a ritual of human sacrifice. Tanner's feet dragged. He almost turned and bolted, but Bridgett's voice cut through his fear.

"Just remove your clothes and hop on the bed."

Struggling for balance, Tanner laughed. "Sounds like an interestin' invitation."

"Tarzan, *monami*, I'm more woman than you can handle. Save the come-on for Jane." She smiled to take the sting out of her words.

Not a complete stranger to disrobing in front of women, Tanner still felt at a distinct disadvantage in front of Bridgett. Hell, with arms like hers, she could have been a wrestler.

He slipped out of his jeans and pulled off the shirt, tossing them both on the chair behind his desk. Fighting the urge to cover his privates, he perched on the edge of the raised cot. "Are you sure this will hold me?"

"*Oui*, it's held women bigger than you with no problem. Come, *cheri*, we only have fifteen minutes 'til you're due to go on. We'll need time to apply the makeup and time for it to dry. Here, wear this." She handed him an eye mask.

"What's this for?" He glanced at the little black mask and then to the woman. "You're not going to blindfold me and paint me like a rainbow, are you?"

"I'll have you know, I take my work seriously. It's my calling card—the reason people come back—they love my sense of style."

"Yeah, yeah, just make me look like Johnny Weissmuller, and I'll recommend you to every Tarzan wannabe I come across."

Unable to avoid the inevitable any longer, Tanner settled the eye mask over his forehead and into place, and then lay back against the cushioned headrest. As relaxed as he could get with Brumhilda about to run her hands all over his body and a camera crew waiting to zoom in on Tanner in a loincloth. There had to be a limit to what a person had to do to make a sale. He felt so...so...cheap.

Tanner heard the sound of a cap being removed and something being squirted. Then he felt cool lotion being smeared over his neck and chest in a firm, yet gentle motion. Almost as good as a massage. Tanner's muscles relaxed. It didn't even bother him when she worked her way down to his loincloth. Her hands were professional and efficient.

"Time to turn over." Brigett stepped

back so Tanner could maneuver onto his other side.

"Damn, I'll have to go to my car for the other bottle of tanning lotion. It'll only take me a minute. Wait right here." Before Tanner could say anything, Brigett dashed from the room.

Like he'd go anywhere else with only half a tan. He probably looked like a half-baked chicken or a pancake that hasn't been flipped. Great, and the door was unlocked. Since the lights were off, he didn't think anyone would venture in, so he relaxed and waited for Bridgett to return.

She wasn't gone from the room more than a few minutes when Tanner heard the door open, announcing her return.

"That was fast. What did you do, sprint?"

"Uh, yeah," she spoke in a whisper, like she was reluctant to wake him if he'd fallen asleep.

"Let's get this done, I'm due on the set in just a few short minutes. If I'm not on time, Janine will think I wimped out."

"Oh, she won't. I promise."

Chapter Nine

Janine had been searching for Tanner since she'd arrived at Peschke Motors, only no one had seen him for the past twenty minutes. After checking with the receptionist, Janine headed for Tanner's office, bumping into a lady carrying a tube of lotion going in the same direction.

"Excuse me, I was just looking for Tanner," Janine said.

"*Oui*, you must be Jane." The woman had sported a painfully fake French accent. She stuck out her hand. "I'm Bridgett, zee makeup artist assigned to bring Tanner's tan up to par with Tarzan. I'm so excited to meet you. You're a real celebrity, you know."

"Thank you." Janine cheeks heated. "But commercials aren't really what I call acting. And by the way, my name is Janine."

"Oh, *pardon moi*," Bridgett said. "I saw you two on zee talk show last Saturday, and I thought you were *manufique*. You really did, how do you say, back him into a corner with zee loincloth dare."

"Yeah." Janine had been feeling a bit guilty about that. "I was actually looking for him to tell him I wouldn't think any less of him if he didn't wear the outfit."

"No, no, don't do zat." Bridgett flapped her hands. "You should see him wearing zee loin cloth, with zee tanning lotion and all. If I were a younger woman, I'd be all over him." Then as if she just remembered, she jumped. "*Sacrebleu!* I cannot stand around here talking, I have zee other side to finish before he goes on."

Janine's pulse had jolted into overdrive as she recalled how he looked in the dressing room. "Could I sneak a peek?" she asked.

"Girlfriend, I'll let you finish the job, if you want." Bridgett's mouth curled in smirk. "He has zee nerve asking you to wear zat outfit when he would not wear one himself. It would serve him right for you to finish zee job without him knowing it."

Butterflies cartwheeled in her belly. "Do you mean it?"

"*Oui!*" Good as her word, Bridgett had shoved the fresh tube of tanning lotion into her hands, giving her the minimal instructions necessary, then sent her into the lion's den, or office in this case.

Seeing Tanner lying on his stomach, his face turned away, gave her the courage to advance all the way into the room. She was squirting tanning lotion on her hands when he spoke, and she almost squeezed the entire contents of the tube clear across the room.

"So what do you think of the

commercials?" Tanner asked.

Lowering her voice and adding the fake French accent, Janine responded, "It is *manufique.*"

"No, really. I'd like your honest opinion." Tanner lifted his head in an attempt to look through his mask in her direction.

Panic flipped in her gut. She shoved his head down and applied lotion to his back while scrambling for an answer to his question. "All of Austin eez watching. It must be a good indication of zee attention you and zee beautiful Jane are getting."

"That's the idea." Tanner's voice was muffled against the padding of the portable bed. "Did you like the monkey and the snake?"

"Zee monkey yes, zee snake no," Janine answered honestly. "Why don't you let your partner have more say?"

"I planned on it for this one. Don't tell her I said so, but she's built to be in front of the camera."

Janine's hand stopped smearing the lotion, and she felt a pang of guilt for listening into a conversation he thought he was having with Bridgett.

"Built as in a natural for film?"

"I guess, but I was thinking more of, you know, built. Legs that could stop a train, curves that never quit and a pair of—Ouch!"

"*Sacrebleu*, I am most sorry." Janine wasn't sorry at all.

"I didn't think applying tanning lotion was supposed to include being pinched." Tanner reached up to pull off his mask.

Janine tugged his hands back down to his sides. "You must be still until zee tanning lotion is completely dry, *monsieur*."

"Yes, ma'am," he said.

Janine clammed up and went to work to finish the job Bridgett had started. She didn't realize how much rubbing lotion on a man's back could stir her senses. Having worked primarily on the shoulders, she forced herself to move farther down his back to the edge of his costume riding low on his hips. She accomplished the journey in slow steady strokes, but she was breathing hard by the time her fingertips ran into the fabric of the loincloth. Just a scrap of material was all that was there, separating her from his sexy tush.

"Don't forget the backs of my legs." His voice startled her out of her wicked imagination, only for a second.

When Janine glanced down at his legs, she could see where Bridgett had left off. She would have to smear lotion from his ankles all the way up to...She gulped and squirted lotion onto her fingers. Starting at the farthest point, she worked the tanning cream into his ankles and up his calves. Muscles bunched then loosened as her fingers worked their magic.

Janine kept a tight leash on her hands, but her mind hopped leaps and bounds ahead of her actions. What would it feel like to touch her lips to the backs of his thighs? If this stuff was edible icing instead of tanning lotion, would he be as turned on as she was and maybe let her lick it off?

She was now up to the backs of Tanner's knees with her own mind turning to mush. A little farther and she'd have it all done. More lotion on her hands and she was working her way up the outsides of his thighs. That was safe enough, but she still had one more area to cover. By now, her cheeks must be flushed. Reaching over his leg, she ran her hands up the insides of his thigh, pushing upward to the edge of his costume almost touching his—

A hand shot out and grabbed hers. "That's close enough. I'm sure the camera isn't gonna zoom in there."

Janine checked his eye mask. Whew! It was still in place, and he probably still thought Bridgett was doing the tan.

"I must say, you do a helluva job applyin' tanning lotion, Bridgett." Tanner shifted on the table.

"Uh, *merci*," Janine said.

"Are you available on Saturday for a repeat performance?"

Janine's lips tightened. Why the arrogant

so and so! "No, no, *monsieur*, I do not date clients." She squirted more lotion on her fingertips.

When her fingers met with his back, he jumped. "I thought you were done with that stuff."

"*Oui*, only a few spots zat needed a touch up." She worked quickly to finish the job, adding icing to the cake or insult to injury depending on your point of view. Dropping her fake French accent, Janine smiled then smacked him on the fanny. "There now, Tarzan, you look more like you belong on that commercial with me."

"Janine?" Tanner sat up and pulled off the mask, all in one motion.

Dropping the empty tube, Janine sprinted for the door, leaving a confused Tanner struggling to get off the collapsible bed.

Metal squealed.

Janine turned back in time to see the middle of the bed buckle.

* * *

After struggling for a few minutes to free his finger from the collapsed portable bed and get to his feet, Tanner threw a sheet around his mostly naked body and dashed out the door after Janine.

What was she thinking playing games with him? She'd invaded his privacy and lied about who she was. He slowed a little as he recalled her hands smoothing lotion on his back and up his thighs. Knowing it was Janine made a big difference. Bridgett was nice, but Janine...

As he traipsed through the showroom in nothing more than a sheet, Tanner was the object of many good-natured catcalls and general harassment from the salesmen.

"Hey, Tanner, I thought this was a jungle theme, not a Roman toga party. If I'd have known, I'd have worn mine."

"Woooohoooooo! Look at those legs."

"Kinda hairy if you ask me."

Tanner glared in their direction and, without a word, headed for the car lot and Janine. He had a bone to pick with her. Who did she think she was, sneaking into his office and pulling a stunt like that? And to think he had been ready to declare his love to the magical fingers of Bridgett when it had been Janine all along.

As soon as he stepped through the doors of the showroom and out into the car lot, he was pounced upon by one of the camera crew. "Where have you been? We were practically frantic. You only have a minute to get in place. Hurry."

"But—"

"No buts, you need to get over there by Janine and the elephant. And for godsakes, lose the sheet. You look more like Julius

Caesar than Tarzan. And one more thing, we only have the one microphone, so you'll have to hand Janine the mike when it's her turn to talk."

Commercials had been the only places Tanner had ever felt confident and in control, until today. Shoved into place next to the towering elephant, Tanner wore nothing more than the equivalent of his underwear. He struggled to get his bearings.

"The elephant's name is Fifi." The trainer stood beside him.

"Fifi? What kind of name is that for an elephant? I'm supposed to say 'Down, Simba' not 'Down, Fifi'." Irritation tightened his jaw. "What kind of Tarzan do you take me for? All of Austin will be laughin' out loud."

The trainer gave him a sideways glance at the brief costume. "Don't go blaming it on the elephant. Besides, the wife named her and that's all she goes by. If you want to get her attention, you'll have to call her Fifi."

"Fifi." Tanner tugged at his too-tight loincloth. "Great, I'm wearin' an outfit no self-respecting Texan would be caught dead in, and my co-starrin' elephant's name is Fifi."

"I think Fifi is a lovely name." Janine patted the elephant's trunk.

A tap on his shoulder had Tanner turning around. "Huh?" Fifi's trunk waved in his face, snuffling his hair, searching for hay or whatever elephants ate.

Tanner frowned, pushed the trunk aside, and tried to unwrap the sheet from around his body. "Janine, could you keep this oversized poodle from interferin' so I can get naked for the camera?"

"You're the commercial mastermind, you figure it out." She crossed her arms across her Jane-clad breasts.

Damn, the woman was sexy. Even when she was mad. "We need to talk." He gave her a brief, pointed look.

Finally, he loosened the end of the sheet from where he had tucked it. A waft of warm air blew across his back, and the next thing he knew the elephant had grabbed the sheet from around him and yanked it clear. Since he was still wrapped, the motion spun him until he was completely free of the fabric.

His hands, microphone and all, automatically assumed the fig-leaf position as Tanner's face burned.

The cameraman yelled, "You're on!"

Cursing a thousand curses in his head, Tanner took a deep breath, lifted the microphone to his lips, and attempted a smile.

"Hi, I'm Tanner Peschke of Peschke Motors back to tell you about the huge savings you'll get when you buy a used car from Peschke Motors. Are you feeling exposed—"

Fifi nuzzled Tanner's neck, distracting him from the lines he'd memorized. "Down, Fifi," Tanner hissed to the side, then into the mic, he smiled and continued, "—exposed to high-pressure sales talk and deals that make you want to trumpet your frustrations?"

Apparently, Fifi liked the smell of the tanning lotion. The tip of her trunk sniffed at his back, waist, and now she was going for his legs.

Batting at her trunk, Tanner looked over at Janine for help.

One corner of her mouth lifted with the corresponding eyebrow. Then she patted the elephant and whispered into her ear.

"Join me, Tanner," he pounded a fist to his chest and swung his arm toward Janine, "and my ever helpful assistant, Jaaaannnnne!"

Fifi dipped her trunk beneath Tanner's loincloth and goosed him. When he jumped and yelled Janine's name, the elephant looped her trunk around his middle and tried to lift him from the ground.

Tanner was no longer in any semblance of control, and the film was rolling on live television.

"Down, Fifi!" he yelled, as the elephant swung him gently back and forth with him wrapped in her trunk, his back to the cameras. "So help me, if you don't put me down, there will be no peanuts for you, girl."

Tanner's gaze searched through a sea of moving faces for Fifi's trainer. He spied Janine, doubled over, clutching her sides alongside his chief of sales, Scott. Fuck. They were laughing.

They were absolutely no help. How was he supposed to finish the commercial when he was being held hostage by a crazy man-eating elephant?

Janine grabbed the microphone from Tanner's hand and stepped toward the camera, schooling her face into a smile. "Join Tarzan and Janine at Pesky Motors for Saturday's Elephant of a Sale."

"Peschke," Tanner yelled, hanging from elephant's trunk. "Hey, get me down!"

* * *

Joe stood in his living room, punching numbers into the cordless telephone and maneuvering the remote to the television simultaneously. What he wanted to press was the volume button, but he realized it was the redial button on the phone. "Damn."

The phone on the other end of the line rang once, twice—"Beans, you watchin' this?"

His friend's slow drawl answered, "Yep. Never thought the boy had the *cajones* to wear a getup like that on public television. You sure you're ready to hand that dealership over to him? Looks like more of a clown than a businessman."

"I know exactly what you mean, but I'm still bankin' on that case of beer. I think he'll pull off this thing, yet."

"Based on tonight's show, I'm betting it's mine."

"Hey, what's that written on Tanner's back?"

"Don't know, cain't quite make it out."

The line was silent as the two men moved closer to their televisions to check it out.

"Looks like two words," Joe said, his head swaying with the elephant's tempo.

"First two letters are M and E," Beans said.

"What's the rest? My damned eyes are gettin' worse every year. Remind me to see my eye doctor."

"Don't forget to see your eye doctor. Looks to me like the next three letters are T-A-R."

"M-E-T-A-R?"

"The next letter looks like a very sick Z. And the last two look like A and N."

"What does it mean, M-E-T-A-R-Z-A-N?"

"Don't know, but the boy's usin' every bit of advertising space by the looks of it."

"That's my boy." Joe shook his head, and sighed. "Suppose he'll get down from that elephant alive?"

"If not, you can get me that case of beer sooner."

Chapter Ten

"Great job, Tarzan." Scott held out a towel.

"Thanks." Tanner was not believing for a minute Scott meant what he said. How could he? The commercial didn't go according to his plan and once again, all of Austin would be laughing at Tanner Peschke.

"Don't worry, your reputation will recover eventually." Scott clapped a hand on Tanner's naked shoulder and quickly drew it away to examine it. "That stuff doesn't come off, does it?"

"I don't know. Fifi didn't show any signs of tanning lotion on her trunk and I'd say she held on a little tighter than you did." Tanner rubbed his sore ribs where the elephant had grabbed him for a good fifteen minutes. The trainer had a heck of a time convincing her to let go. Something in the tanning lotion made her determined to hang on to Tanner, no matter what the trainer said or did.

The camera crews left as soon as Tanner was out of any danger and no longer an interesting subject to the general public. He searched the dwindling crowd for Janine, but she was nowhere to be seen.

"If you're lookin' for Janine, she left as

soon as the elephant let go of you."

"I wonder why she left so soon? I wanted to talk with her."

"That's probably why she left in such a hurry." Scott settled in the chair behind Tanner's desk.

"Why?"

"I would, if I was the one who wrote that on your back."

"Wrote what?"

"Me Tarzan." Scott pressed his lips together into a thin line and rose from the chair. "You mean you didn't know?"

"Know what?"

"Never mind." Scott dug in his pocket for his keys, edging toward the door. "Guess I'll be goin'."

Tanner stepped in front of him. "You're not goin' anywhere until you tell me what the hell you're talkin' about."

"Uh, Tanner, old buddy, old pal..."

Scott dragged it out to the point Tanner wanted to strangle him. He narrowed his eyes to a slit.

"You've been had. Your makeup artist told me all about it."

"All about what?"

"Janine."

"What about Janine?" His hands curled into fists.

"Come with me." He led Tanner through

the empty showroom, stopping long enough to dig a compact mirror out of the receptionist's desk drawer, then marched Tanner to the men's restroom. Once the door closed, he turned Tanner so his back was to the mirror and handed him the compact. "Look and see for yourself."

Completely frustrated with Scott's vague innuendos, Tanner looked into the compact at the back of his head. "So?"

"Don't look at the back of your head, dufuss. Look at your back." Scott tipped the mirror in Tanner's hand.

Then he saw it. In bold, tanning lotion block letters were the words "Me Tarzan".

"Why that—"

"Now Tanner, it was an innocent prank."

"Innocent, my big foot. I've gotta find her."

"She left."

"Then I'll go to her apartment." Tanner twisted to reach the letters on his back with the towel.

"Here let me try." Scott took the towel from Tanner. He soaked a corner of the terry cloth in warm water and rubbed at the offending letters.

Tanner watched through the compact mirror. "Well? Did any of it come off?"

Scott paused to look at the towel. "Sorry, buddy, none of it's coming off. I think it has to wear off."

"Let me at her." Jaw clenched tight, Tanner pushed Scott aside and strode through the showroom. The inside lights were out and the lot outside had cleared. With the exception of one huge pile of something.

"Hey, what's that in the middle of the pavement?" Tanner peered through the glass doors. Unable to identify it, he tossed the towel over his shoulders and stepped outside. The stench assailed his nostrils before he got within ten feet of the mystery substance.

Scott held his hand over his nose. "Looks like Fifi left her calling card."

"Why did the trainer leave it here?"

"Come to think of it, cleanup *was* specifically mentioned in his contract," Scott said.

"Then why didn't he do it?"

"That's the problem. I recall somewhere in the fine print, that you are responsible for all cleanup." Scott grinned and lifted a hand in farewell. "Have fun."

"I'm responsible?" Tanner gaped at the reeking pile of elephant dung. "Who am I gonna get out here at this time of night to clean up this mess?"

Scott was halfway across the lot before he answered, "Well, boss, I have to get home. I have a roast in the crockpot."

"You don't even own a crockpot, nor

163

would you know how to use one. Get back here and help me with this."

"Sorry, boss." Scott slid behind the wheel of his SUV and rolled down the window. "It's not in my contract to clean up after elephants who aren't properly car-lot-trained. See you tomorrow. You know, you better have that gone by mornin'. The odor could take a bite out of sales."

Tanner chucked the towel at Scott's retreating vehicle. Why did it seem the more he tried, the deeper he got? Soon, he'd be in over his head and that stunk.

* * *

The phone was on its seventh ring by the time Janine got her door unlocked. Something about a phone ringing on the other side of the door that set her on edge. That feeling of knowing someone might need you and you couldn't get to them fast enough was all she could figure.

But tonight, Janine hoped the instrument would stop ringing before she could answer it. She didn't feel like talking to anyone, especially this late. All she wanted was a shower and a cup of tea.

She dropped her purse and keys on the hall table and lifted the phone to her ear. "Hello."

"Oh my god, Janine. Saw you on that Pesky Motors commercial tonight. You were superb."

"Thanks, Monty." Janine cradled the cordless phone on her shoulder and walked across the small living room to the only bedroom in her efficiency apartment. She really didn't want to talk to her agent at this hour. Monty tended to go on and on about what she could change to land a gig. "Do you realize it's almost eleven-thirty? Why are you calling so late? It's not like you."

"I was so excited by your performance tonight, I called a friend back in L.A. I think I may have an audition lined up."

All fatigue vanished before Monty finished his sentence. "Really?" Her pulse raced, but she tried not to let herself get too excited. She'd had hundreds of auditions and had yet to land a decent role. But none of the auditions had been in L.A.

"Yeah, really. It's for work in commercials. At least you'll be getting your face seen out in L.A.—if you do it."

Janine's balloon deflated. "Commercials?"

"Not everybody walks into the job of their dreams the first time out. At least, this will get you bill-paying work and your face seen by more of the people who count in the movie industry."

"But Monty, I don't want to do commercials the rest of my life. I want to do serious acting." Her shoulders slumped. "You know that."

"I get you the auditions, the rest is up to you and the casting director. You have to build up some credits. Doing makeup conventions isn't getting you seen by producers."

Janine kicked her shoes in the direction of the closet, and she ran a hand through her hair, shuffling the phone to the other ear. "I know, Monty. It just takes so long to break into the business. If something doesn't happen soon, I'll be playing Juliet's mother instead of Juliet."

"Hang in there, Janine. I'll call as soon as I get more details."

"Okay, Monty. I appreciate all you've done." Janine pushed the off button, and dropped the phone on the bed. So much for big breaks. She trudged into the miniscule bathroom and turned on the water in the shower.

Why did chasing your dream have to be so difficult? The roller-coaster-ride of emotions wore on her stamina and she began to doubt her choice of careers. Perhaps she should be glad and settle for commercials. The work put bread and butter on the table. Granted, commercials in Austin versus commercials in L.A. would be a little different.

Janine stripped out of her Jane outfit and stepped under the shower spray, mentally listing the pros and cons.

If she went to L.A., she could possibly be in commercials on national television where the casting agents had more of a chance of discovering her than in Austin, Texas. Of course, the cost of living would practically eat her alive. That had been one of the deciding factors for staying in Austin all this time. She wasn't sure she wanted to suffer like so many other starving artists trying to break into the movie industry in California.

At least in Austin, she could afford an apartment by working part-time doing commercials and conventions. The odd part she landed in the theatre was a step in the right direction for her acting career. But at the rate she was progressing, she'd be dead before she was discovered.

Janine turned off the water and wrapped her hair in a towel. Monty was right. She should be in Los Angeles or New York City. Austin wasn't getting her where she wanted to be.

Perhaps the thought of leaving Austin was what held her back. This was the town she'd been raised in since she could remember. She was comfortable here. She knew the city like the back of her hand. What did she know about L.A. other than what she'd learned by studying maps and brochures acquired via the Internet?

Other than her mother, she didn't have any family left in Austin and her friends weren't really close. So what was keeping her here? If asked that question a month ago, she'd have said nothing.

An unbidden picture of Tanner flashed through her mind. What was he doing there? Not as if he was family or a friend. They barely knew each other.

So, they'd fallen into bed a couple of times. Bumbled their way through some hawt kisses. But you couldn't really count those, could you?

Never mind his kisses turned her knees to butter and made her forget her own name. The chemistry didn't mean a thing—at least to Tanner. He was a ladies' man destined to break many hearts. But not Janine's.

A little depressed by her thoughts, Janine rummaged through her dresser, searching for her most comfortable blue flannel pajamas with fluffy white sheep printed all over them. Once she had on the flannels, she fished her bunny slippers from the back of her closet and slid in her feet, immediately feeling better. Something about this outfit made her feel more at home, like she was a little girl again and her mamma had just kissed her goodnight. She wished she could talk to her mother about her confused emotions, but she might not want to hear what Mamma had to say. A friend to talk to would have been nice—someone who understood her struggles...

A knock sounded on the door.

"Now who could that be at this hour?" Someone not a friend, no doubt. Someone who might have a bone to pick with her about the prank she'd pulled. Still, her depression faded. A spark of excitement skittered through her, perking up her attitude. Lifting her chin high, she strode for the door.

Tanner was dog tired, but he wanted to get a few things off his chest before he called it a night. Raising his hand to knock again, he hesitated when he saw something move in front of the peephole. "Janine, it's me Tanner. Let me in."

Nothing like the straightforward approach. He was tired of the games and being laughed at. Hell, he was just plain worn out, beat, bushed, pooped...you name it. Shoveling elephant dung was a physically challenging task. One he hoped never to have to do again in his lifetime. But the job was done and the lot was clean of all evidence of Fifi.

Now, he had to clean up a little matter with Janine—then he could go home, get a shower, crawl in bed and sleep until next month...or tomorrow, whichever came first.

The door cracked open enough for Janine to peek around it. "What do you want? It's late. Decent folks want to sleep."

"Yeah, so do I. But I have a bone to pick with you, and I want to get it done tonight. Are you gonna let me in, or am I gonna have to shout through the door and wake up all your neighbors?"

"Shhh." Janine opened the door a bit more and motioned him in. Once the door was shut behind him, her eyes widened and her nose wrinkled. "What is that smell?"

Tanner frowned. "Fifi."

Janine's eyes widened. "You brought the elephant with you?"

"Yeah, she's waiting in my car." He jerked a thumb over his shoulder then shook his head. "Of course, I didn't bring the elephant. I spent the last hour cleaning up elephant sh—poop."

"Oooh, that doesn't sound like very much fun." Janine covered her nose. "Tanner, you really smell bad. Couldn't we talk tomorrow? After you've been fumigated or something?"

"No, I want to talk now."

"Would you like to use my shower first? Really, you're making me gag."

His flagging strength revived a bit, his

libido kicking up a notch at the thought of Janine and a shower. And he really did smell bad. Tanner sighed. "Fine. But what will I do for clothes?"

"I have a bathrobe hanging on the back of the door. Leave your clothes outside the door, and I'll stuff them in my washer."

Too tired to argue, he followed her all ten steps through her tiny apartment to the bathroom. Once inside, he shed his jeans, shirt, and the offensive loincloth. Once naked, he slipped the clothes around the door and stepped under the warm spray of water in the shower.

Ahhhh. Heaven. He searched for a bar of soap, finding only shower gels and liquid soaps smelling of flowers and herbs, just like Janine. Squirting a liberal amount of lavender-colored goo on his hand, he worked it into lather all over his body. Suddenly, the scent mixed with the hot water and he felt completely surrounded by Janine. With his eyes squeezed tightly shut to keep soap from entering them, he could clearly see Janine as she'd been the first day he'd met her. Sitting astride the mechanical bull, rocking to the motion of the machine. How he'd envied that bull... Tanner groaned.

"Are you all right in there?" Janine's voice carried over the spray of the shower.

No, I'm rock hard with no sign of let-up. "I'm

fine," Tanner said through clenched teeth. He rinsed soap from his face and turned off the hot water, the cold water dousing his red-hot reaction to Janine's scent. It helped, but not much. As soon as the frigid water was off, his desire reasserted itself. *I'm stepping out of this bathroom to chew out Janine while sporting a hard-on in her fuzzy pink bathrobe. Tanner Peschke, my man, you've indeed sunk to a new all-time low.*

Why was he there? Oh yes, he was mad about the writing on his back. Checking in the mirror, he reaffirmed it was still there. Somehow, the anger he'd felt earlier had washed away with the soap. So, he should just put on his clothes and leave. But that's not what he really wanted to do. He wanted to be around Janine. She made him laugh at the things she said, the way she said them and most of all, at himself.

She was everything he wasn't. Her motivation to succeed in something she loved doing was inspirational. But what he admired most was that she knew exactly what she wanted. Somehow, Tanner knew she would get it. That would mean leaving Texas for either California or New York, but she deserved to live her dream.

So where would that leave him? In Austin, selling cars for Peschke Motors. The thought took the starch out of his sail to the point he felt he could walk out of the bathroom in the pink fuzzy robe and not embarrass himself.

He sucked in a deep breath and opened the door, stepping through the bedroom where Janine would later lay sleeping. He tried not to look, but the thick floral comforter and piles of pillows drew his gaze.

He remembered every moment he'd spent there, reclining, propped against the headboard, completely naked, Janine's full breasts beckoning him with hardened peaks.

His ship set sail again and his mast jutted out before he reached the living room. Conducting a sharp about-face, he almost escaped unnoticed. Almost.

"Feel better?" Janine stood in front of the couch, holding a mug. Her hair spilled down over her shoulders, still damp and curling softly. The lack of makeup only made her look younger, softer, even more appealing. Her flannel pajamas fully covered her body except where they crisscrossed at the opening of the lapel, exposing a tantalizing glimpse of her bountiful boobs.

The total affect was excruciating.

"Yes, I feel better," he lied through his teeth.

"You smell infinitely better." Janine smiled. "Would you like a cup of tea?"

"I'd prefer a beer."

"I just so happen to have one." She rose

and headed for the kitchen.

Tanner took a seat on the couch, pulling and tugging on the bathrobe, determined not to draw attention to his heightened awareness of her.

The television was on, the sound down low. While Janine worked in the kitchen behind him, he concentrated on the late-late news. Maybe a good dose of robberies and drive-by shootings would lessen his leaping libido. But concentration was at a minimum with the object of his desire only a few steps away.

"Oh, my gosh," Janine said from behind him.

Tanner stared down at his tented lap and covered himself with a throw pillow, his face burning. He glanced up and behind him with a sheepish grin on his face.

Janine wasn't looking at him but at the television.

While he had been lusting over Janine, the late news was showing clips of their earlier attempt at a commercial. "Can you turn it up?" Tanner stood.

Janine grabbed for the remote, increasing the volume.

"Tanner Peschke and Janine Davis have set the city of Austin on fire with their crazy commercials and hilarious antics. Tonight's fiasco with the errant elephant is only one example of the unique commercials produced by Peschke Motors. Each commercial leads the entire city to the question, 'What will they do next?' We will keep you posted with news clips and interviews with the talented Tarzan and Jane of Peschke Motors in Austin, Texas."

The news droned on, but Tanner and Janine remained in awed silence for a few seconds. Gazing into each other's eyes, they both burst out laughing at the same time.

"Can you believe it?" Janine's eyes sparkled.

"I counted two mentions of Peschke Motors. Wow, that should boost sales. If it doesn't, I don't know what to think."

"Did you hear? They got our names right." Janine bounced on the balls of her bare feet, hugging herself around the middle.

"We did it." Tanner grinned. "We killed two birds with one stone."

"What's that?"

"We got your name and face on television, and more free advertising for the dealership."

"Not bad for a day's work, huh?" Janine gave Tanner a high five.

Instead of a brief contact, Tanner entwined his fingers with hers and tugged her closer. "You're amazing, Janine Davis."

"I am?" She blinked up at him, her voice

breathy.

"Yes." Tanner's gaze dropped to her lips, his head descending to claim them.

"Are you going to kiss me?" she breathed.

"Yes." He pressed his lips to hers, pulling her hand close to his chest, and wrapping the other around her lower back to pull her hips against his.

What started as a light exploration of touch, quickly graduated into a flaming tangle of thrusting tongues and groping hands.

Janine's fingers pushed inside the loose ends of the pink robe, finding his chest, and feathering through the damp hairs.

Tanner's pulse thundered, pushing blood south as his hands moved lower, cupping her cute little derriere, pressing her closer to his hardened arousal.

He fingered the buttons on her pajamas, loosening them to let her shirt hang open so he could drink in her naked beauty. His head dipped and took one glorious rosy nipple fully into his mouth.

A loud buzzing sound filled the room.

He freed her breast. "What was that?"

Janine struggled to answer, her swollen, very kissed, lips working to form words. "The dryer. Your clothes...they're done."

"To hell with the clothes. I want you, Janine. All of you."

The dryer's buzzer seemed to have ruined the moment for Janine. From soft and pliant, she stiffened and pushed him away, pulling the sides of her shirt together.

"Please, you should go."

"But why?"

"Just go, will you?"

What was going on? "Will I see you again?"

"Yes—no—oh, I don't know." She pressed her fisted hand against her mouth, her eyes pooling with unshed tears.

Not wanting to upset her further, Tanner grabbed his clothes from the small, stacked dryer, and beat a hasty retreat to the bathroom. Once dressed, he emerged to find Janine waiting by the door.

"We need to talk," he said.

Janine's face was clear of emotion. "Not now. I want to be alone."

"Okay, this time. But we will talk."

She pulled open the door. "Goodbye, Tanner."

Tanner winced at the tone of finality. "Not goodbye. Goodnight. I'll see you tomorrow."

Chapter Eleven

What was she thinking? Kissing Tanner like they had a future was totally and completely insane. What about her dreams, her goals, her career?

The same thoughts plagued her, destroying her sleep. The hollows under her eyes looked like sunken half-craters on the moon. Tugging the Jane outfit into place, Janine kept a furtive eye out for Tanner. The sale was going well, and he was busy meeting the customers, media and all the curious people of Austin who'd stopped by to see if he was all right after the elephant incident. She couldn't have gotten close to him if she'd wanted.

Which was just as well. What would she say? *Sorry, Tanner, but last night's kiss was a mistake*—or—*Don't get any ideas, I have a plan and you're not in it.* This was all assuming Tanner was interested in more than a brief kiss.

Janine noted the flock of women bent on getting his autograph.

He smiled at each of them, the smile that curled her toes the first time they'd met. Face it, Tanner loved women and they loved him.

She would end up as just another notch

on his bedpost.

So? What would it hurt to have an affair with him? Would doing so change her plans? No. Would the sex keep her from realizing all her dreams? No. Then what was the problem?

Janine shook her head and looked at Tanner. He picked that moment to glance up and grin her way. Was he thinking of last night? Janine felt her cheeks burn with the memory. They had been so close and she could have fallen into bed with him so easily. A stab of regret hit her like a punch in the gut. Maybe skipping breakfast was all that was wrong with her. A bagel would fix that right up.

What would having an affair with Tanner get her? A few days of magic, some fond memories to carry with her to L.A. So what was she afraid of?

Losing her heart, and a bagel wouldn't cure that. The answer came unbidden in her thoughts. No, it couldn't be that. Janine hadn't planned on ever losing her heart as her mother had. That choice had only landed them in the poor house with unfulfilled dreams and a hundred regrets. Love wasn't worth it. It was a gamble that never seemed to pay off. Someone would fall out of love and she'd be left paying the debt the rest of her life.

No, love was not for Janine. The emotion

wasn't in the plan. Ever since she could remember, she'd had stars in her eyes. There wasn't a time she didn't have her goals set to make it to the stage or film.

Janine glanced up, her eyes narrowing with determination. She couldn't, wouldn't let a little thing like falling in love stop her. *Be strong, don't sway.* Then she saw Tanner pushing his way through the crowd toward her. Her resolve melted in that instant, and she did the only thing she could.

She turned and ran.

* * *

"Okay, Monty, I'll fly out for the audition a week from Monday. I have a commercial to shoot this Friday, the sale on Saturday, then I can be on a plane Sunday night. That sound all right?"

"Peachy, just peachy. You won't regret this, I promise. It's only the beginning of a fabulous career," Monty said in his usual flamboyant style.

"Yeah, okay, whatever you say." Her mind on Austin and the Tarzan who'd walked away with her heart, she barely paid attention to her agent. "Look, Monty, I've got to get some rest. Can we discuss the details later?"

"Sure thing. Give me or my secretary a call any time this week, and we'll have everything you'll need."

"Great. And Monty?"

"Yeah?"

"Thanks," she said. *Thanks for getting me out of here.* Janine pressed the off button on her phone and flopped down on her couch. For a woman with the opportunity to move to the city she'd always longed for, she sure wasn't jumping up and down in excitement. What was wrong with her? Here was a legitimate chance to start fresh and pretty darn close to her dreams. Why couldn't she muster more enthusiasm?

Hugging a flowered throw pillow to her chest, she closed her eyes and envisioned Tanner as he'd been last night in nothing but a pink fuzzy bathrobe. Damn even in that, he'd been sexy. How could she resist such a man? She sank sideways on the couch and half-heartedly punched the pillow. *I'm doomed.*

When had it happened? When had she actually fallen in love with a used car salesman? How could she let herself do that? Hadn't she learned anything from her mother's miserable life? Janine felt a lump invade her throat.

* * *

I love her. Oh, my god, I love her.

The thought came to him when he saw the determined look on Janine's face cascade into desperation just before she'd hightailed it off the car lot.

What was that all about? She sure was

acting strange and it was about time he got to the bottom of her behavior.

Surrounded by customers, salesmen and his new fan club, Tanner couldn't break through to reach her in time. She'd gotten away. Every fiber of his being screamed to follow her. He'd been in the process of disengaging from the people surrounding him when his father arrived.

Tanner watched in amazement as the crowd seemed to part for the commanding presence of Joe Peschke.

"Tanner, my boy, let's go inside where we can talk."

"I'd love to Dad, but can it wait?" Tanner asked, glancing around for a glimpse of golden hair, but she was already unlocking her car.

"No, son, I have a few things to get off my chest. No time like the present."

Tanner gave one last look in Janine's direction. She was in her car and headed off the lot. He'd never catch her. But he'd find her after this meeting with his father.

As he followed his father through the showroom into the back offices, his mind strayed to the woman driving away. He had the sinking sensation that the farther away she drove, the less chance he had of getting her back. But that was absurd. Where would she go? To her apartment on the west side of

Austin? Not so far he couldn't get there in under thirty minutes. Taking a few deep breaths, Tanner braced himself for the four-hundredth lesson in the Tanner series.

"Now, son, I can't argue with the sales figures. The other part of the business is maintaining a professional presence in the local car sales circles," Joe Peschke began.

"Yes, Dad." Tanner settled into a seat beside his father's desk. At least from this location, he could look out the window. He'd learned that trick long ago in a similar meeting. In an attempt to get comfortable, he shifted in the chair. This could go on for a long time, and he'd much rather be in pursuit of one beautiful woman.

"I understood the need to save the monkey and the girl from the boa constrictor. But this latest bit with the elephant only left you looking like a fool."

"Yes, Dad." Tanner nodded at the appropriate points to indicate he was listening, even when he wasn't.

"It might be all right for the marketing manager of the dealership," Joe swiveled his chair. "But the president and owner can't go around acting like a clown on television without becoming the laughing stock of the town."

"But Dad, we'll be laughing all the way to the bank."

"Quite so, quite so, but that doesn't erase the impression this dealership is being run by a bunch of clowns. If you ever want to expand and possibly go into the new car market, the manufacturers'll be lookin' at the whole package. They'll wanna know their products are bein' taken seriously and sold by competent dealers." He waved a hand toward the window. "Do you see where I'm goin' with this?"

"Yes, Dad," Tanner said, automatically, then thought again. "I mean no, Dad. What are you sayin'? You want me to take over and build this business into something bigger than it already is?

"That's always been my dream, son. And if you start out in the right direction, you can make it happen."

Tanner had to take a moment or two to get a grip on the rampaging thoughts racing through his head. His father wanted him to take over the dealership some day. That was a given. Having been brought up with that thought drilled into his head since he was old enough to say *Have I got a deal for you*, Tanner knew this was the plan his father had for him.

But expanding the dealership into selling new cars and possibly opening more locations? The noose around his neck tightened, and he reached up to loosen his necktie. "Whoa, Dad. Wait just a minute.

Who said anything about building this business bigger? I'm not so sure I want to do that."

"Nonsense. You can't halt progress. In order to make a livin' at this, you've gotta think big and expand or be taken over by the competition."

Tanner stood and paced the length of the room. "Dad, we have a hard enough time makin' a profit at this location. How in the heck do you think I have what it takes to make a go of even more locations?"

"I'm convinced you can do it, son. Just look how you turned yourself around in just a few short weeks. I know you can expand with a little guidance in the management arena."

"Dad, I appreciate that you have confidence in me." And Tanner really did like that his father now believed in his abilities, but…"I need to think about what I want out of the business."

"Well, don't think too long. I'm really considerin' handin' over the business soon, and I want to know your heart is in it."

"Like I said, Dad, I want to think about this. Give me some time."

"Take some." His father swept his arm wide, then ended with a finger pointing Tanner's direction. "But not too long. In this business, if you snooze, you loose…millions."

His father's words followed him enroute

to Janine's apartment. Spotting a flower shop, Tanner swerved into the parking lot and bought a beautiful bouquet of red roses. On his way out, he noticed a pet store with a white fuzzy kitten pawing at the window as if waving to get his attention. That's all it took was one wave of the kitten's paw and he had to have it for Janine. The puffy thing reminded him of her, all soft and feminine just made to be loved and cuddled.

Once in the car, he removed the bright red bow from the vase of roses and tied it around the kitten's neck. "There, can't have you goin' to a new home without a welcoming ribbon." As he drove the rest of the way to Janine's apartment with his carload of bribes, he scratched the fur ball behind the ears. How could a woman turn away a man bearing such gifts? And he really wanted her to let him in. More than anything he'd ever wanted in his entire life. More even than his father's approval.

Chapter Twelve

Janine tossed and turned, deep in the throes of a bad dream. She'd been riding along a dark road with sheer drop-offs on both sides. As she topped a steep incline, she strained to see over the crest, discovering she couldn't see because nothing was on the other side. Before she could stop herself she was falling, falling, falling into a black abyss with no hope of ever being found.

"Tanner!" Janine reached out, hoping he'd find her and save her before she was lost forever.

Thunk. Pain shot through her head and hip, meaning she'd hit the ground and she was still alive, not lost in an abyss. Janine opened her eyes to stare up at her coffee table. She wasn't on a rickety highway or falling into a bottomless pit. Instead, she was lying on the floor next to her couch, clutching a wrinkled throw pillow.

A strange scratching sound came from the direction of her door.

She hauled herself to her feet, mentally counting the bruises she'd just acquired. *Who could be at my door in the middle of the n*—Janine glanced at the clock on the mantel—*day? Wow, was it only five o'clock in the evening?* Disoriented

187

and cranky, she wasn't in any mood to entertain, nor buy anything from some persistent salesman. "Go away," she called through the door.

The scratching stopped, and she thought her entreaty had worked its magic. Good. She turned toward her kitchen and a cup of tea, when...

Scratch, scratch, scratch.

Janine dragged her fingers through her hair and swung back toward the door to peek through the peephole. The little bit of hallway she could see was empty.

Scratch, scratch, scratch.

Leaving the chain in place, Janine unlocked the door and looked out. "Whoever's scratching on my door better quit it. I've got 9-1-1 on speed dial, and I'm not afraid to use it."

The hallway was as empty as it had appeared in the peephole. Then she felt something soft curl against her ankle, and she almost jumped out of her skin. "Yeek!!!!"

She leaped to the chair situated next to the table in the entryway and stared down at the floor, expecting to see a huge rat or snake or something equally horrifying. Instead, a fluffy white face looked up at her, its head tipped to the side.

"A kitten? What the heck were you doing out there?" Janine stepped down off her perch, scooped the kitten into her arms, unlocked the chain, and stepped through the doorway.

Standing against the wall was a pair of jean-clad legs with a bouquet of roses for a face. Then Tanner Peschke peered around the flowers and smiled. "I see you found Rocky." He gestured toward the kitten.

"Rocky?" Janine cocked an eyebrow at the purring fuzz ball licking her fingers. "Oh, the kitten?"

"Yeah. I thought it only fitting that a male kitten that looks like a powder puff should have a tough name. You know, to keep all the other cats in the neighborhood from pickin' on him. Don't you think so?"

His eyes widened like a little boy, so hopeful. Janine had mixed signals from her mind and body. On the one hand, how could she resist a good-looking man wielding flowers and a kitten? On the other hand, where did her dreams and career goals fit in with the Tanner picture? Her pulse rate quickened with one glance at his lips and breathing became more difficult. Memories of their last kiss assailed the feminine hormones taking control of her body. She pressed the kitten to her face to hide the warm flush spreading through her cheeks. "What do you want, Tanner?"

His smile slipped a little, but then

returned in full force. "Is that any way to treat the rescuer of small animals?"

"You rescued this kitten?" she asked.

"Yes, from a cold display window or possibly some family with mean little boys." His grin stretched his firm mouth. "A fate, I'm sure that's worse than death. So you see, I'm a hero."

Janine rolled her eyes.

"Rocky thinks I am, anyway. Don't you, Rocky?" Tanner stepped closer to tickle the kitten's furry neck. The gesture brought his hand close enough to brush against Janine's breast.

Her indrawn breath was a borderline gasp and alerted him to her awareness. He looked up to gaze into her eyes. The flames of desire leapt in his, searing her with their heat.

Janine stumbled backward, putting distance between her and Tanner. But the space wasn't enough. As she stood inside her apartment with him on the threshold, she felt trapped. "I can't do this, Tanner."

"Do what, Janine?" His words were low and sexy. He stepped toward her, closing the distance she'd created. With careful deliberation, he laid the flowers on the table by the door, lifted the kitten from her arms, setting it on the floor, and, in the same motion, closed the door behind him. "Can't love me?"

"No." Janine twisted her fingers together, now that she didn't have the kitten to keep her hands occupied.

"Why?" He separated her hands, bringing them to rest against his chest.

How right they felt there. She could feel his heart beat through the cotton of his chambray shirt. Not slow and steady like his advance on her. But every bit as erratic as hers. Somehow, this little bit of information pushed her over the edge, and her fingers inched up around his neck, pulling him down.

Tanner's hands slipped around her backside and pulled her hips firmly against his. Evidence of his desire nudging her belly, enflaming her body and setting her blood on fire.

She couldn't get close enough. Her breasts pressed firmly to his chest, the tips hardening against the lacy fabric of her bra.

Their lips touched, tentatively. Janine drew back, licking her lips as she stared at the firm set of his mouth. The touch wasn't nearly enough.

She moved closer and he bent his head, waiting.

Who was she kidding? Certainly not him, with his lips beginning to curve as he hovered.

Rising on tiptoes, she placed her mouth against his, giving him another soft press of lips. Their mouths opened, sweet hot breath brushed over her, and she was lost. The kiss she gave him next moved past chaste pecks to thrusting tongues in seconds, matching the primal motion of their mating hips.

Meow. Rocky rubbed against her ankle several times before Janine came to her senses. She pushed against Tanner's chest, backing up until his arms dropped their hold around her.

"This is going way to fast." She touched her fingers to her lips, shaking her head. "I can't love you, Tanner. Don't you see?"

Her eyes met his, tears blurring her vision. But there was no mistaking the smile on his face or the understanding in his eyes. "Yes, I do see." He pulled her close again, resting her check against his chest and brushing a kiss across her forehead. "You have a dream, a career, something that means more than staying here in Austin. I know that, and I'm not asking you to give it up."

"You're not?"

"No. I love being with you. I love the way you talk and walk and...well...everything about you does funny things to me. I can't help wanting to be around you. If it's only for a few hours, days or weeks, I'll take what I can get."

"And when I leave?"she asked, her voice quavering with emotion.

"No strings. I'll let you go." He tipped

her chin so she could look into his eyes and see the sincerity written there.

"You won't be hurt and hate me?"

"No, I won't hate you." He kissed the tip of her nose. "I'll thank my lucky stars I got to be with you for the time I had."

Janine remained quiet. Her logical self told her to have a little fun. What could it hurt? When the time came to leave, she'd have some great memories and still have her career.

Janine's heart screamed that she was a fool. A career couldn't love her or snuggle with her when she was cold and scared. Nor could it fire her blood and make her want to toss her inhibitions out the window for a lifetime of passion and caring.

An image of her mother came to mind— careworn and tired from working two jobs to support her daughter. What dreams she'd dreamt had been crushed out of her by the reality of life. Janine couldn't let herself go down that path.

"I'm not asking you to give up anything."

Tanner's words broke through her inner turmoil.

His fingers stroked her hair. "I only want to be with you while I can."

Janine straddled the fence. Should she go along with his suggestion and enjoy this while it lasted? Or was it too big a risk to her heart?

"I tell you what," he said in that low rumble, "we'll take it slow. Let me take you out for dinner where there are people all around, and you won't feel pressured by being alone with me."

Rocky meowed and stood on his hindquarters, his front legs climbing Janine's pants.

"What's the matter, little guy?" Janine squatted on her haunches, buying time to think. When she came back up with the kitten tucked under her chin, she'd made up her mind. "Dinner sounds nice, but let's call out for pizza. I don't want to leave Rocky alone on his first night in his new home."

Life was short, why deny the attraction? She could pick up the pieces of her broken heart after she'd relocated to L.A.

Tanner fought the urge to shout out loud. She had invited him to stay. There really was a God and he was alive and well in Austin, Texas. The prayers Tanner had sent His way had worked, and he was going to spend time alone with Janine, in her apartment. What more could he ask?

A little dark cloud rolled in and sat over Tanner's happy thoughts. Unfortunately, Tanner wanted a lot more than one night with Janine. If he thought there was any chance he could make her happy, he'd ask her to marry him and stay in Austin to be the wife of a used car dealer.

In the next moment, he shoved aside that thought. He couldn't ask her to do that. She had dreams, and he wanted her to follow them and make something more of herself than Austin could provide. With her talent and beauty, she'd go far in Hollywood. Who was he to throw a wrench in her plans? No, better to do as he'd said. Take what he could get and deal with her absence later.

Instead of proposing, Tanner ordered pizza, while Janine dug through her refrigerator unearthing a couple bottles of beer. What a woman. No frou-frou wine coolers for her. She kept beer. He was definitely in love, and she was perfect for him.

Too bad, he couldn't follow her to L.A. Being the only heir, Tanner was stuck with the family dealership. Besides, he would only hold her back. Hollywood wanted young, single actresses they could market to the world, having love affairs with other actors. What would she want with a used car salesman? Not that he needed money. He had enough and then some to afford his own place out there. Tanner didn't see himself as Mr. Janine Davis or fitting into the Hollywood scene.

Besides, she hadn't asked him to come with her or follow her wherever she went. Clearly, Janine wanted to make it on her own.

He'd better get used to the idea he'd lose her eventually. The thought sat like a bone in his craw. He had to get used to the idea, but he didn't have to like it.

While they waited for the pizza to be delivered, Janine fished out plates and napkins, and Tanner set the small table in the kitchen. Moving between the table, cabinets and refrigerator was tight and they bumped into each other, often...probably more than necessary, but who was counting? Janine was soft and feminine and Tanner couldn't help it. He had to touch her.

Janine set a bowl of milk on the floor in front of Rocky.

The kitten plunked a paw in the middle of it and lapped as fast as his tiny tongue could go.

Janine leaning over to pat the kitty was a sight Tanner would remember forever. Her glossy blond hair spilled down her back and across her face, her soft pink sweater stretched tight over her curves.

He would have fallen to his knees and taken her into his arms. But the floor was hard tile and his kneecaps were not what they used to be before high school football. Instead, he squatted at her side and tucked a strand of hair behind her ear.

"You're beautiful, Janine Davis." He kissed the tender skin beneath her earlobe, and then Tanner straightened and offered her a hand, pulling her into his arms. "I'm going to kiss you, although I know I should wait. Seems like every time we do, something interrupts us. I'll bet the piz—"

Janine shut off the flow of his words by sealing his lips with hers. Hands groped for buttons, loosened tucked shirts, and unzipped in a flurry of motion. Luckily, Tanner had a spare condom in his wallet, and, between the two of them, they rolled it into place.

In less than two minutes, Janine was naked and sitting on the edge of the kitchen table, dishes pushed to the far corner, her legs wrapped around Tanner's waist. She threw back her head and clutched at his hair as he thrust deep inside her, again and again.

Tanner shook his head, a little amazed at how fast things had moved. While he was poised to erupt, he doubted she was on the verge, and he didn't want to mess this up. He pulled away, ignoring her mewling complaint and tightening thighs.

Bending over her, he planted his elbows on the table and thrust his hands into her silky hair. "Let me catch my breath."

Her eyes widened, then squinted into a glare. "I thought you were in better shape."

"I'm in great shape, as you and the rest of Austin's viewing audience are only too aware. But I'd like to use a little more finesse, sweetheart. Make this memorable."

"I'm spread out on a scratched wooden table. How much more memorable can you make it?"

He smiled at the grumbling texture of her voice, at the way her nose wrinkled up in disgust. "Seems like we've skipped a few preliminaries. Gone straight for the goal."

"Again, I don't see the problem?" But her mouth curved into a smile, and she flirted from beneath her long lashes.

Maybe she protested a little too much. Arguing only seemed to make the pretty rose color of her cheeks deepen.

"Want to move this to the bedroom?"

"I kind of like being dessert."

"We haven't eaten dinner."

"Exactly." Her grin sank a dimple deep into her cheek.

Tanner swooped down and kissed it, then trailed his lips along her cheek, kissed her chin, then a dozen little spots between before he bent over the crest of a round breast.

The nipple was a lovely, puffy cone of sweetness, which he proceeded to lap up like strawberry ice cream. Her fingers sank into his hair, her thighs climbed his sides, soft heels digging into his back. When he latched his lips around the tip and sucked, her back bowed off the hard wood table, then her fingers dug deep, directing his head across her chest to the other ripe tip.

When he'd savored her surrender for several delicious minutes, he let go of the tight little bead and moved downward.

Her breaths shortened, her skin quivered as he nipped at her ribs, delved into her belly button. He propped her thighs on his shoulders and growled as he dove between her legs, eliciting a nervous giggle, then a long, deep moan.

She tasted like the sea. Salty and fresh. Her folds were moist, fragrant, tasty. He said so, which earned him a clap across the top of his shoulder.

Smiling, he didn't mind that he'd embarrassed her, loved that she seemed to find the pleasure he gave her something unexpected. Perhaps her wholesome figure and smart mouth were a little misleading. Not that he minded if she had a little less experience than he expected.

He'd have liked to have all her firsts. Be the best she ever had. So she'd never forget him.

But the shivering of her thighs and jagged breaths told him she was close, so he rose, waiting as she moved to clasp his waist again, then settled the head of his aching sex against her entrance, and drove inside.

This time, they were both there. Both trembling with arousal. He moved slowly at first, inching his way forward until she'd taken everything he had to give, then easing out again.

However, Janine didn't seem to like his caution. She pinched his buttocks, raked her nails across his back. "Move, Tanner. Please, God, *move*."

The strained quality of her voice rather than her words was what convinced him. He cupped her buttocks, lifting them off the edge of the table and powered into her, his motions quickening, sharpening, then slamming deep.

Janine's arms floated to the table, her eyelids faded down, her mouth rounded as she made little kitten-like sounds, that grew wispier, more desperate.

Tanner widened one palm to brace her, then slid the other hand around front and burrowed a finger into the top of her folds, circling on the hard little nubbin there until her eyes slammed open and she gave a strangled scream.

Only then did he let go, allowing the pressure in his balls to erupt as he dove into her, again and again. When the last pulse of pleasure waned, he withdrew and dragged in a deep breath, becoming aware of his surroundings and the woman watching him intently from below.

Tanner was amazed by the normalcy of the scene after what he'd just experienced with Janine. He stood in the middle of a compact kitchen. The kitten had finished its milk and was curled up on Janine's pink sweater. Napkins had fluttered to the floor. Someone knocked on the door.

The door.

"Ohmigod, the pizza delivery man!" Janine's face flamed.

In unison, they broke apart and grabbed for their clothes, knocking heads together and laughing. Tanner hopped down the hall, sliding one leg at a time into his pants.

"Just a minute," he called through the door. Tanner fished in his back pocket, searching for his wallet. Not there. "Janine, have you seen—" He turned toward the kitchen and stopped in mid-sentence.

She stood right behind him, holding the wallet in her hand, wearing nothing but a smile.

Tanner's heart stopped then sped on. In that moment he knew, she was the one for him. He plucked the wallet from her fingers as if her hands were dangerous, and boy-howdy were they. "You can't answer the door like that," he growled, then shoved her behind the door.

Shirtless and a little flustered, Tanner opened the front door a crack. Just as he suspected a pimple-faced, teenage delivery boy stood tapping his toe with an insulated pizza bag held over his shoulder.

With the pizza boy on one side of the door and a naked Janine on the other, Tanner was so befuddled he dropped his wallet. When he bent to retrieve it, feminine fingers reached out and pinched his ass. Startled, he came up so fast he hit the pizza bag, flipping it high into the air to land upside down on the floor.

"Man, like that pizza's toast." The teenager shook his head as he picked it up. He pulled the box out of the bag and opened the lid. Pepperoni and cheese stretched down from the top of the box. "Yeah, it's a mess. Want me to get you another? If you'll let me use your phone, I'll call back to the store and—"

"No, no. That one will be just fine." Tanner stuffed a couple bills in the boy's hands and grabbed the box. "Thanks."

Tanner slammed the door in the pizza boy's face, sailed the box across the room, and lifted Janine into his arms. There were better things to do than eat pizza.

Chapter Thirteen

The next morning, Tanner drove Janine to the airport after staying up the entire night.

"I won't be back until noon on Friday, and I expect to be busy the entire time. So I might not be able to call." Janine determinedly set Tanner's expectations up front so he wouldn't be waiting around the phone for her call.

"Break a leg, my sweet Jane." He held her close one last time. "I'll see you when you get back."

"I'll be there for the next commercial, Tanner," she promised.

After a poignant goodbye kiss, Janine made her way to her economy-class seat next to the window. She could see Tanner standing at the window of the terminal, scanning the length of the aircraft until he spotted her. He smiled and gave her a thumbs-up. Knowing he was rooting for her made her warm inside, and at the same time, she felt cold without him close by.

Damn. What was she going to do? She'd lost her heart to an Austin car salesman. That was the last thing she'd intended to do. Maybe this trip away would put things in perspective, and she'd find that distance was all she needed. By the time the plane pulled away from the terminal and Tanner's smiling face, Janine wasn't so sure her plan would work out quite the way she'd hoped. Time would tell.

The flight was long and boring, which was just what she needed to catch up on a little of the rest she'd missed during the night shared with Tanner. Janine drifted off to sleep with a smile on her face, recalling the gooey pizza they'd peeled off the box to feed to each other in the wee hours of the morning. Nothing had ever tasted so good.

* * *

Tanner paced the showroom floor, checking his watch. He proudly wore the Tarzan outfit in anticipation of the weekly Peschke Motors commercial. All he needed was for Janine to show up to be his Jane. Everything else was ready, and they only had about thirty minutes until the cameras rolled. Where was she?

"You're as jumpy as a caged animal." Scott leaned against a shiny pre-owned Corvette. "Have you heard anything about Janine's flight?"

"I called an hour ago. The airline said her flight had been delayed. How late could it be? She was supposed to be here at noon." His hand scraped through his hair. "I hope she didn't get stuck in Denver. They had a heck of a storm stirring over Colorado."

"What's your backup plan if she's a no show?"

Tanner shrugged. "I don't have one. This whole concept depends on her being here."

"The concept...or the man is dependant on her being here?"

Tanner stopped and glared at Scott who immediately raised his hands to ward off Tanner's anger.

"Okay, okay, it's none of my business. But this is the first time I've seen you go ape over a woman. Allow me the pleasure of laughing just a little."

"There's nothing to laugh about." He rolled his shoulders to dispel some of the building tension. "She's supposed to be back by now."

"As unglued as you are now, how are you going to react when she leaves for good?"

"I'll deal with that when and if the occasion arises."

"Buddy, it's a given, you should accept it and move on." Scott patted Tanner's back. "Janine's headed for the bright lights and big city."

"I know." Tanner's chin almost touched his chest. "I've always known it, but that fact doesn't make it any easier."

"Hey, monkey man, why so glum?" a heavenly voice floated from the doorway.

"Janine." Tanner's entire world lit up the

moment he laid eyes on her wearing her Jane costume. Two giant steps had her in his arms, crushed to his chest, and swept into a deep soul-wrenching kiss. Holding her so close, he had delusions of never letting her go.

"If you don't mind, I'd like to breathe," she gasped, laughing at his exuberance. "You sure know how to make a girl feel missed."

Scott cleared his throat. "Hi, Janine,"

"Hi yourself," she said around Tanner's arm.

"I hate to be the bearer of bad tidings and the one to break up this charming reunion, but you have about five minutes to get into place and read your lines."

"So what's the animal flavor of the day?" Janine pushed a stray strand of hair off Tanner's forehead.

Damn, she looked good. Tanner's tongue had to be hanging out because he felt he could lap her up like a dehydrated beast would water. "Flavor?"

"Animal?" She raised an eyebrow. "You always have an animal in the commercial. You aren't changing things on my account, are you?"

"No, no." Tanner shook his head to clear it. "We have a camel tonight. I wanted something that wouldn't hurt you or cause any problems. The trainer assures me Sheik is as gentle as a lamb."

"Sheik, is it? Well, let's get out there. We have a commercial to do."

"But how'd it go? Did you get the job?"

"No time to talk now. We can discuss it later. I see the cameraman waving."

Tanner and Janine stepped out of the showroom into the night air and joined the camera crew and the animal trainer. Sheik stood placidly chewing his cud, unconcerned by the lights and noise of the people around him.

The trainer tapped the camel's knees with a stick and the beast collapsed into a sitting position. "Climb on board, Miss Davis."

"Climb on?" Janine smiled at Tanner. "Surely you don't expect me to ride that?"

"Actually, that's the idea." Tanner grinned. "If you don't mind, it'll only be for a minute."

Janine glanced at the boxy seat precariously strapped to the one-hump of the dromedary. "He won't toss me, will he?"

"No, Sheik is as tame—" the trainer began.

Janine finished his sentence, "—as a lamb. I know. I've heard that one already—from a monkey trainer. Well, here goes nothing." She dragged in a deep breath and climbed into the seat.

The animal trainer clicked his tongue, and the camel lurched forward climbing to his feet where he stood towering over Tanner with Janine even higher.

Tanner frowned up at Janine. "I didn't realize he'd be so tall. You sure she's okay up there?"

"As safe as a baby in a car seat," the trainer assured him.

"Don't you hurt her, you hear," Tanner threatened the camel.

The animal tossed his head as if mocking the measly human standing beneath his chin.

"One minute," cried the cameraman.

"Are you all right up there?" Tanner called up to Janine.

"Just fine. Since I'm so far up here, I take it I don't need to worry about lines."

"I'll take care of it." He loved that her attitude was light and flexible. "You just concentrate on holding on."

"Not a problem. I have a death grip on this crazy seat."

A shout from the cameraman caught their attention. "Five, four, three, two..."

"Hi, I'm Tanner Peschke of Peschke Motors. Does finding a dependable pre-owned car feel like trying to find an oasis in the middle of a desert? Then ride along with Janine and drop on by Peschke motors where we'll quench your thirst with the car of your dreams." Tanner swung his arm wide, turning to face the camel and the girl. "Join—"

Before he could finish his words, Sheik spit a slimy green stream of salivated hay square in the middle of Tanner's face.

Completely taken off guard, Tanner stumbled backward, landing in the front seat of a BMW convertible and leaning heavily on the horn.

He scrubbed the slime from his eyes in time to see Sheik's eyes roll back in his head. The camel backed away from the blaring car, yanking the frantic animal trainer off the ground with the force of his exit.

"Tanner!" Janine screamed from atop the frightened camel, which only scared the beast more. Jerking the reins out of the animal trainer's hands, Sheik plowed through the crowd of onlookers, toppling camera-laden tripods, scattering people right and left.

Tanner struggled to get out of the convertible, leaping after the lumbering beast. Too late. Sheik was well on his way down the busy streets of Austin with a screaming Janine hanging on for dear life.

"Call 911! Call the fire department! Call someone! Janine'll be killed if we don't stop that camel." Tanner jumped into the convertible whose horn pushed the camel over the edge then honked and beeped his way out of the busy car lot to chase after the runaway and his hapless rider.

Within a dozen blocks, he caught up to

the speeding camel, but there wasn't much he could do to stop him. So he followed along behind him, his gaze glued to Janine who flopped back and forth with each clumsy lurch.

I'm so sorry I got you into this, Janine. If—when we get you down from there, I promise to never put you at risk again. Tanner sent a prayer to heaven to take care of Janine. She didn't deserve to die or have all her bones broken because of his clumsy mistakes. She was everything to him and when he got her back down, he intended to tell her so.

If she left afterward, that action was okay but he had to tell her. Just in case a smidgen of a chance existed she would change her mind and stay. He'd do anything to keep Janine in his life. Even tackle a camel if he could.

Before long, Tanner could hear the screaming of sirens as no less than a dozen police cars converged on the street, taking up positions in the chase. They too kept a healthy distance from the camel, probably just as unsure of what to do as Tanner was.

Then the wop-wop-wop of rotary blades pierced his consciousness and looking up confirmed the presence of the eye-in-the-sky helicopter. Holy shit! A police escort and the helicopter? All for Austin's darling of the jungle, Janine Davis. Despite his worry,

Tanner smiled. He was so proud at how well she held on and stayed with the animal. When this was all said and done, she'd fare well with the public. How could she not?

Several miles from the dealership, Sheik's jerky pace slowed. Tanner crawled behind them in his convertible and finally slammed the vehicle into park and leaped out of his seat. The camel was too busy heaving for air to notice when Tanner grabbed his reins and tied them to a nearby signpost.

Sheik didn't argue. He was totally exhausted and immediately knelt and settled down to rest. Tanner was glad because he didn't know the commands to make the animal get down. He wasn't sure he could catch Janine if she were to jump from that high up.

"Janine, honey, are you all right?" He reached up to help her out of her seat.

"I don't know." Janine crawled off the seat and stood on terra firma. Her knees buckled. "Oh, Tanner. I was so scared."

Tanner grabbed behind her legs and lifted her into his arms. "Shhh, baby." He pressed kisses to her eyes and cheeks, followed by a deep one to her lips. The television news crews were already in position, capturing the entire ordeal on tape to be aired on every channel in the vicinity of Austin.

But Tanner didn't care. He had Janine

safe and sound, and he wasn't going to let go any time soon.

* * *

"Well, Beans, I believe you can pay me that case of beer." Joe Peschke clasped his hands behind his head and leaned back in his recliner. "I'd say that pretty much clinches his chances of makin' a profit. The dealership will be positively hoppin' with happy customers following that spectacle."

Beans shook his head and gave Joe a sideways grin. "Gotta admit, I ain't seen anything like that in all my born days. You got somethin' special in that boy, and he'd be a fool to let that Janine go."

"Doesn't look like he's going to. Do you think they'll pass out kissin' that long?"

"Don't know, but what do you say about double or nothing, they do?"

"Nope, my bettin' days are over," Joe said with a shake of his head. "Can't imagine toppin' this one and I make it a habit to quit while I'm ahead."

Beans chuckled. "Can't say's I blame you. Nope, can't blame you. Think he'll up and marry that woman?"

"He'd be a fool if he didn't," Joe replied. "Come to think of it, I wouldn't mind a few grandkids around the place. When I retire, I'll have loads of time on my hands. I wouldn't like anything better than to teach my grandchildren how to fish."

"Since when have you been fishin'?"

"I haven't," Joe said. "But that's something I plan to rectify as soon as I turn over the dealership to Tanner."

Beans snorted. "You'll never give up the business. "It's in your blood. You'd die without it."

"But that's the beauty of turnin' it over to Tanner. I can get a work fix whenever I feel like it."

Beans gave him a narrow-eyed glance. "That's assumin' he wants it."

Joe's chest deflated. "Quite right. Guess I won't know until I ask the boy."

"Yeah," Beans said. "Aren't they havin' the World Wrestling match on at eleven?"

"As a matter of fact, seems I saw something like that advertised. Give me the remote."

"*I'll* drive." Beans snatched the remote out of Joe's reach.

Chapter Fourteen

Janine waited around the phone all morning for Tanner to call and finally climbed into the car. She would stop by the dealership to return the Jane outfit. That was as reasonable an excuse as any, she figured. Besides which, she wanted to gauge his reaction to the news that she'd be leaving for L.A. permanently. Would he be broken-hearted or relieved? If last night was any indication, his reaction would be the former.

Then why had he left without a word before daylight while she was sleeping? The adrenaline rush they'd both experienced after the runaway camel incident fired passions worthy of the Guinness Book of World Records. Janine's skin warmed at the memory, and she stared at her reflection in her rearview mirror. No, she was still the same Janine, even after such mind-altering sex.

The muffled sound of Janine's cell phone chirped from the depths of her purse. Would it be Tanner? Eager to answer, Janine kept one hand on the steering wheel, digging blindly with the other to locate the persistent device. Her hand was close because the vibrating battery was rattling her fingernails.

"Ah ha!"

Success was short lived when the light in front of her turned red, and she slammed on her brakes to keep from running through the intersection. She dropped the phone in the process and spent the length of the light fishing around on the floorboard for the pesky thing. It better be Tanner Pesky or she would throw it out the window after such an ordeal.

Taking a calming breath, she punched the receive button and smiled into the phone. "Hello," she said in her sweetest, come-hither voice, anticipation making it slightly breathy.

"Janine, Monty here."

Her heart plummeted into her stomach, and she fought to control the urge to hang up. Of all the people she least wanted to talk to right now, Monty was number one on the list. What a turnaround that was. For the past year, not a single day had gone by she didn't race to the phone, hoping Monty called with the news she'd been waiting for—a part in a play, a reading for a movie script, an interview with a casting director.

What was so different about today?

She'd been away from Tanner for almost a week and last night's reunion was absolutely magical. That's what was different.

The thought of moving to L.A. had lost most of its appeal since she'd met a particular car salesman. Was it worth it to move all the way across the country just for a career? What about love, marriage, and raising a family? Her mother's words made more sense now. Augh. Had she really thought that? After years of swearing off those institutions, was she seriously considering settling down with a car salesman?

"Janine? Are you there?" Monty asked, his voice rose to compensate for the sporadic static of cellular systems.

"Yes, Monty, I'm here," she replied.

"Are you sitting down?" he asked.

Looking around the interior of her car, she smiled and shrugged. "Yes, Monty, I'm sitting."

"I've got a bonafide offer resting here on my desk for you."

"They want me for the commercial?" she asked, less than enthusiastic. If she was going to do commercials, she'd rather do them here with Peschke Motors.

"Nope." Monty paused.

The hesitation went on so long he apparently waited for her to guess. Janine frowned. All the way to L.A. to audition for a commercial and they didn't want her? Impatient to see Tanner and tired of playing games, Janine snapped, "I give up, I have no idea what you're talking about."

"Janine, my girl, you've been offered a lead in a series."

A series? Janine's heart jumped into her throat and threatened to explode out the top of her head. Swerving to miss a cyclist, she struggled to get a grip on her emotions.

"A series?" she asked, stupidly.

"Yes, your very own series. Can you believe it?"

"No, it's absolutely unbelievable." Janine missed the turnoff for the dealership, she was in such a state of moronic delirium. She veered off the road into a restaurant parking lot, and took several deep, cleansing breaths before asking, "A lead part in a series?"

"Yes! Isn't it wonderful? I'm so excited for you I can hardly stand it. I can just imagine how you're feeling."

"Frankly, I don't know what to feel," she whispered. "This is like the fulfillment of all my dreams, the pinnacle of my existence, the ice cream on the cake. Unbelievable..." She clicked off the phone and stared into space. Then for good measure, she reached across her chest and pinched the opposite arm. Nope, she wasn't asleep even though she hadn't slept most of last night because she and Tanner—

Excitement bubbled up inside. Inaction combusted into action, and she slammed her car into reverse, backing out of the parking lot and spinning a donut in the middle of the road to go back a block to Peschke Motors.

This news was too incredible to keep to herself. She had to tell someone. And that someone had to be Tanner.

* * *

Being with Janine last night had been every bit as terrific as he'd remembered from their last time together, which made getting up and leaving her before daybreak all the harder. Tanner had too much on his mind, and dragging Janine down with his concerns wouldn't be fair. So he'd left early to return to his apartment to change into jogging shorts and tennis shoes. He needed activity to clear his brain and jogging usually accomplished that.

At twenty-eight years old, he should have his life figured out and a direction chosen. But he'd been lulled into thinking that direction had already been decided since the day he was born. There was no choice in the matter. He would take over his father's business and that was that.

Tanner jogged through the streets of Austin, climbing hills and dodging stray cats. The more he ran, the more his muscles screamed. Strangely, the pain numbed, and with the numbness, a clarity of vision magnified his life into full-blown realization. The decision *wasn't* made, he really had choices he could make in his life.

At the same time this epiphany occurred,

the sun came up, spreading a bright orange light of hope across the city.

After spending years coasting on the expectations of others, Tanner realized he was the one who had to take control of his life. He had to make his own decisions, good or bad. With this in mind, he picked up the pace until he sprinted all the way back to his apartment. Barely winded, he took the steps two at a time, arriving at his door breathless but full of hope.

After a quick shower, he was back out the door and driving away to the dealership. He had work to do and no time like the present. Hitting the auto dial for his father, he waited while it rang three times. "Come on, Dad, pick it up."

"Joe Peschke speaking."

"Dad, could we meet at the dealership this morning as soon as possible?"

"I'm glad you called, son, I was just about to leave the house," he said. "We have a lot to discuss."

"Yes, we do," Tanner agreed. "I'll see you there in fifteen minutes."

Twenty minutes later, Tanner had just completed his tenth lap of pacing around his father's desk. What was keeping him?

Another glance at his watch, and he missed his father's arrival.

"Well, son, I have to hand it to you. Last

night was the best yet. I even saw the news report on CNN." Tanner's father smiled, shaking his head. "You're the only person I know who can pull off a stunt like that. I'm proud of you."

With his own thoughts on the tip of his tongue, Tanner paused when the impact of his father's words sank in. "You're proud of me?"

"Yes, I am. I have to admit I didn't think you'd stick it out in the car business. I had been entertaining the idea of selling the store and retiring. Now, I'm glad I didn't. With Scott as general manager and you as the marketing director, this place will be growing by leaps and bounds."

"It will?"

"I have no doubt. Son, the business is yours."

Tanner mentally staggered. The old feeling of carrying the weight of family expectations descended in full force. His dad was finally proud of something he'd done. How many years had he waited to hear those words? Twenty-eight, to be exact. Was the wait worth it?

"So what do you say, Tanner? Do you want the dealership?"

Tanner turned away and walked to the window where he stared out at the rows and rows of shiny used cars. All this could be his, all he had to do was say the word. The glow of his father's approval shone down, temporarily blinding him as he turned to voice his decision.

"Dad, I...can't." Tanner's head hung briefly in mourning for the short-lived appreciation his father'd had for him.

"Can't?" Joe asked, a frown knitting his brow.

Tanner's chin came up and his voice strengthened. "Dad, I love you more than perhaps you'll ever know. I'm glad you think I'm worthy of running this dealership. But the truth is, I don't like this work. Oh, I enjoy the commercials and advertising, but I'll never make a good salesman or general manager and that's what you really need. So, to make a long answer short...thanks, but no thanks."

A sad look settled over Joe Peschke's face for a brief moment, but soon disappeared. "I can't say I'm not disappointed."

"I'm sorry Dad, but—"

The older Peschke held up his hand. "Let me finish, son. I'm disappointed because I'd like to keep you around. But I never really thought you were happy here. So, given all that, I understand and support your decision one-hundred percent."

"You do?" His voice shot high and he cleared his throat. "But what about your retirement? Are you going to sell?"

"As a matter of fact, I had a back-up plan. I wasn't sure you'd want to stay so I asked around and found someone interested in runnin' the shop on a rent-to-own basis."

"Oh, really? And who is that?"

"Scott's been itchin' to own this place ever since I hired him as a snot-nosed salesman, fresh out of college. He's got the drive and the business sense to make this store even bigger and better than I ever could have."

Tanner nodded and smiled, thinking of his friend's abilities and desire to succeed in a business that fired his passion. "He's a good fit, Dad. I can't think of a person better suited."

"Glad you agree." Joe slung an arm over his son's shoulder. "What say you and I go get some breakfast?"

"I'd love to Dad, but I have some other unfinished business—"

"Tanner!" The call could be heard all the way through the showroom floor and into the back office. There was no mistaking that voice—Janine.

"Excuse me, Dad, that's my unfinished business calling." He didn't even bother to look back as he headed out of the office to meet her.

"That's okay, son. Don't let her get away," his father called after him, his chuckle following Tanner to the end of the hallway.

"Tanner Pesky, where are you?" she called.

Stepping out on the showroom floor, he answered, "Peschke. The name's Peschke. What's got you all fired up, pretty lady?"

Before she could utter another word, she launched herself at him, wrapping her arms around his neck in a stranglehold.

"What's wrong?" He held her close, inhaling her perfume and enjoying the close contact. The sensation might not last if she got and offer and moved to L.A. *Don't borrow trouble, Tanner, old boy.*

"Wrong?"

She laughed, the sound like music to Tanner's ears.

Janine leaned back a little, and looked up into his face, a smile stretching from ear to ear. "It's happened. I got a part in a real honest-to-god series." She bounced up and down like an excited child.

A lead ball slammed into the pit of Tanner's gut. He swallowed hard and pasted a smile on his face, pulling her close again on the pretext of congratulating her. If his eyes were a little moist and his voice a bit shaky, she wouldn't notice this way. "That's the best news yet," he said into her hair, breathing in the herbal scent, committing its earthiness to memory. Memories soon would be all he had left.

"I was so excited I couldn't wait to see you and let you know."

"This is terrific. Your ship finally came in." His throat tried to close but he pushed out the words. "It's what you've always wanted and worked for. You deserve it, Janine. I guess this means you'll be going to L.A. soon..."

His words took the starch out of her full-blown sails, and she stopped bouncing to look up into his eyes. The glow in her face faded and tears welled up. "Oh, Tanner," she said. "How am I going to make it without you?"

"You don't need me to make your star shine. Like I always said, you're a natural, they just finally got around to recognizin' it."

"But I don't want to go without you." She wrapped her arms around his middle and buried her face in his shirt.

"Honey." He eased her back far enough to stare down into her eyes. "You've got to follow your dreams. I would only slow you down. And L.A. doesn't need another used car salesman. Besides, my father just offered me the dealership." He crossed his fingers behind his back. Janine didn't have to know he'd turned down the offer.

"He did?" She stared upward, blinking tears from her eyes.

"Yes, he did." Tanner brushed the hair

out of her face and pressed a kiss to her nose. "So you see, I'll have my work cut out for me here while you'll have a few hearts to break in Hollywood."

Janine's tears stopped and a stubborn look descended on her face in a frown. "I'm not going. I'm staying here with you," she said, increasing the strength of her hold around his middle as if to say *just try to stop me.*

"Janine, Janine." Tanner clucked his tongue. "It's the way it has to be—"

"Hey, Tanner, phone call." Scott stood in the doorway of his office.

"Take a message." He glared over Janine's head. "Can't you see I'm busy?"

"The guy says it's urgent," Scott replied.

"Nothing is as important as what I'm doin' right now." Tanner never took his gaze from the woman he loved. He had a mind to kiss her and his lips were halfway down to hers when—

"Tanner, the guy is adamant. I think you need to take this call. It's on line two," Scott insisted.

Tanner frowned at Scott then looked down at Janine. "Don't go away, I'll be right back."

Striding to the information desk, Tanner punched in the line number and answered tersely, "Tanner, speaking." His gaze remained on Janine, afraid she'd leave when he wasn't watching.

"Tanner, you don't know me, but my name is Monty Duet," the man began.

"You're right, I don't know you," he said impatiently. "What do you want?"

"I'm a talent agent working with a company out in L.A. interested in starting a wildlife series. They want you and Janine to be the co-hosts of the series."

"Huh?" Tanner's gaze slipped from Janine to stare at the phone. Was this guy for real? "Is this is a joke?"

"No, no, I'm dead serious. Have you seen Janine yet?"

Tanner looked over to where Janine stood staring out the window of the showroom. "Yes," he answered.

"Did she tell you about the offer to play the lead in a series?"

"Yes," he repeated.

"This is the series I'm talking about. I just didn't have a chance to tell her what it was all about. She hung up on me before I could. Which is probably just as well. I really would rather you break the news the series involves working with wildlife up close and personal. Based on her experiences, I wasn't sure if she'd be as thrilled."

"I understand." A slow smile spread across Tanner's face.

"Well, are you interested?"

"Do I get to think about it?" he asked. Think? Why did he need to think? This was the answer to all his prayers of self-realization. He loved the camera, he loved Janine. He'd have a job he loved, for heaven's sakes. So why was he stalling?

"I need to tell them today, if possible. They want you two out here in two weeks ready to get started."

"Then I have to say...yes. Yes!" Tanner's face split into a huge grin as he hung up. Life couldn't get better. Now all he had to do was break the news to Janine.

"Janine?" He walked up beside her and slid an arm across her shoulder. "Have *I* got a deal for you."

Epilogue

"Can you believe it? My son and daughter-in-law on national television. Who'd have thunk it?" Joe Peschke adjusted the footrest on his chair.

"I always knew he had it in him." Beans stretched out in the other recliner, sipping his beer straight out of the bottle.

"You?" Joe snorted. "If I recall, you were the one bettin' against his success."

"I was bettin' against his success in the car business. I didn't say anything about the film industry."

"Yeah, sure. Now you change your tune, when—"

Beans interrupted. "Turn up the volume. Show's about to begin."

Joe adjusted the volume, and the two men leaned forward.

Tanner, dressed in khaki shorts and a safari hat, stood beneath a huge tree surrounded by vast grasslands that stretched as far as the camera could project.

"Hi, I'm Tanner Peschke, here with my lovely wife, Janine, coming to you direct from the plains of Africa. Welcome to *Animals of the World*. In today's show, we'll discuss the mating rituals of the giraffe and show you the most poisonous snakes of the African continent."

"Snakes?" Janine struggled to keep a smile glued to her face as she hissed out the side of her mouth. "No one said anything about snakes."

"It's okay, Janine, they're just little snakes." He patted her hand and grinned at the camera.

"Honey," Janine said through clenched teeth. "No one said anything about snakes."

About the Authors

DELILAH DEVLIN Until recently, award-winning erotica and romance author Delilah Devlin lived in South Texas at the intersection of two dry creeks, surrounded by sexy cowboys in Wranglers. These days, she's missing the wide-open skies and starry nights but loving her dark forest in Central Arkansas, with its eccentric characters and isolation—the better to feed her hungry muse! For Delilah, the greatest sin is driving between the lines, because it's comfortable and safe. Her personal journey has taken her through one war and many countries, cultures, jobs, and relationships to bring her to the place where she is now—writing sexy adventures that hold more than a kernel of autobiography and often share a common thread of self-discovery and transformation. To learn more about Delilah Devlin, please visit http://www.delilahdevlin.com.

ELLE JAMES aka **MYLA JACKSON** spent twenty years livin' and lovin' in South Texas, ranching horses, cattle, goats, and exotics like ostriches, emus and rheas. A former IT professional, retired Army and Air Force Reservist, Elle is proud to be writing full-time, penning intrigues, comedies and paranormal adventures that keep her readers on the edge of their seats or laughing out loud. Now living in northwest Arkansas, she isn't wrangling cattle, she's wrangling her muses, a malti-poo and yorkie. When she's not at her computer, she's traveling the world, snow-skiing in the Rocky Mountains, boating on the nearby lake, or riding her ATV, dreaming up new stories, characters and adventures. Please visit Elle James at http://www.ellejames.com

Made in the USA
Lexington, KY
18 January 2014